W9-BAQ-312

Cul-de-Sac Kids
Collection One

BOOKS BY BEVERLY LEWIS

Picture Books

Annika's Secret Wish
In Jesse's Shoes • *Just Like Mama*
What Is God Like?
What Is Heaven Like?

Children's Fiction

CUL-DE-SAC KIDS °

Cul-de-Sac Kids Collection One
Cul-de-Sac Kids Collection Two

Youth Fiction

GIRLS ONLY (GO!) ★

Girls Only! Volume One
Girls Only! Volume Two

SUMMERHILL SECRETS +

SummerHill Secrets Volume One
SummerHill Secrets Volume Two

HOLLY'S HEART +

Holly's Heart Collection One
Holly's Heart Collection Two
Holly's Heart Collection Three

www.beverlylewis.com

★ 4 books in each volume   + 5 books in each volume   ° 6 books in each volume

Cul-de-Sac Kids
Collection One

BOOKS 1–6

Beverly Lewis

BETHANY HOUSE
a division of Baker Publishing Group
Minneapolis, Minnesota

© 1993, 1995 by Beverly Lewis

Previously published in six separate volumes:
  The Double Dabble Surprise* © 1993
  The Chicken Pox Panic* © 1993
  The Crazy Christmas Angel Mystery* © 1993
  No Grown-Ups Allowed © 1995
  Frog Power © 1995
  The Mystery of Case D. Luc © 1995

* Originally published by Star Song Publishing Group under the same title.

Published by Bethany House Publishers
11400 Hampshire Avenue South
Bloomington, Minnesota 55438
www.bethanyhouse.com

Bethany House Publishers is a division of
Baker Publishing Group, Grand Rapids, Michigan

Printed in the United States of America

All rights reserved. No part of this publication may be reproduced, stored in a
retrieval system, or transmitted in any form or by any means—for example,
electronic, photocopy, recording—without the prior written permission of the
publisher. The only exception is brief quotations in printed reviews.

ISBN 978-0-7642-3048-6

Library of Congress Control Number: 2017945876

Scripture in The Double Dabble Surprise quoted from the International Children's Bible ®, copyright © 1986, 1988, 1999, 2015 by Tommy Nelson. Used by permission.

Scripture quotation in The Mystery of Case D. Luc and in No Grown-Ups Allowed taken from the Holy Bible, New International Version®, NIV®. Copyright © 1973, 1978, 1984, 2011 by Biblica, Inc.™ Used by permission of Zondervan. All rights reserved worldwide. www.zondervan.com The "NIV" and "New International Version" are trademarks registered in the United States Patent and Trademark Office by Biblica, Inc.™

These stories are works of fiction. Names, characters, incidents, and dialogues are products of the author's imagination and are not to be construed as real. Any resemblance to any person, living or dead, is purely coincidental.

Cover design by Eric Walljasper
Cover illustration by Paul Turnbaugh
Story illustrations by Janet Huntington

19 20 21 22 23   7 6 5 4 3 2

Contents

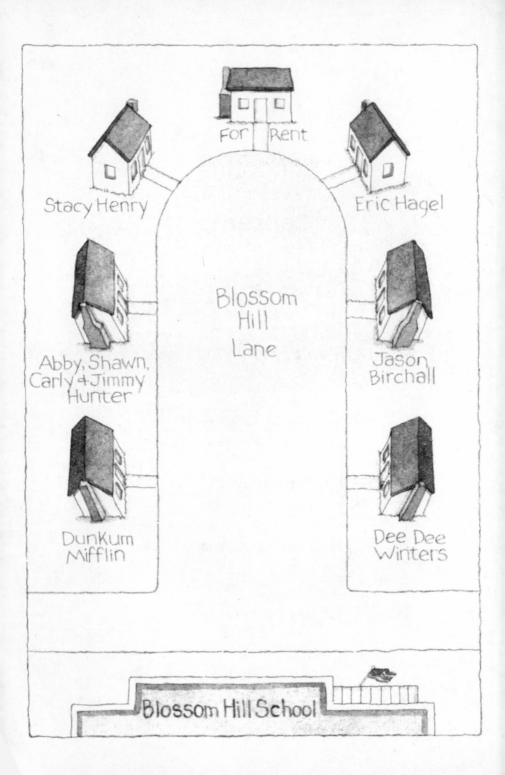

For Rent

Stacy Henry

Eric Hagel

Blossom
Hill
Lane

Abby, Shawn,
Carly & Jimmy
Hunter

Jason
Birchall

Dunkum
Mifflin

Dee Dee
Winters

Blossom Hill School

BOOK 1

The Double Dabble Surprise

To the memory
of my little friend
Skipp Choon Geun,
who now lives in a heavenly
cul-de-sac paved with gold.

One

Abby Hunter drew an X with her red marker.

The X looked perfect on her teddy bear calendar.

"Next Saturday is the *big* day," she said. "In one week, we'll meet our new sisters from Korea."

She made dancing stars around the red X.

"I can't wait," said Carly, her little sister, looking up from her first-grade spelling list.

Abby snapped the cap on her marker. "Just think, there will be four girls in our family."

"I think Daddy wanted some boys," Carly said.

"Mommy doesn't know how to raise boys," Abby said. "There haven't been any boys in her family for three generations."

Carly twisted one of her blond curls. "What's a generator?"

Abby sighed. "Not generator—generation."

"Well, what is it?" Carly asked.

"It's all the kids born in a family. When they get old—about thirty—those kids get married and have kids. Then those kids . . ."

"Okay, I get it," Carly said.

Abby straightened her calendar. "*That's* why we only have girl cousins."

Carly wrote a spelling word. "I'm glad generator isn't on this list!"

"Generation," Abby insisted.

"Whatever," said Carly. She made a tic-tac-toe grid on her paper. "Wanna play?"

"Can't," Abby said. "Dunkum is coming over to shoot hoops."

Dunkum was the best player in Abby's third-grade class. His real name was Edward Mifflin, but no one called him that.

"Dunkum thinks he can't be beat, but I'm trying," Abby said.

"Is Dunkum your best friend?" Carly asked, looking down at Abby's sneakers. One was red and one was blue.

"Maybe," Abby whispered.

The doorbell rang, followed by pounding on the front door.

Abby grabbed her jacket. "That's definitely Dunkum."

Carly sighed. "When our Korean sisters come, maybe they'll play with me."

■■■

After lunch the girls helped their mother put up a pink wall hanging. It read *WELCOME, SISTERS*.

"Soon, I'll have three sisters," Abby said.

Carly jumped up and down. "Just in time for Thanksgiving."

"Before," corrected Abby. "Thanksgiving's in twelve days."

"Carly, please hold your end still," said Mother.

"She's too excited," said Abby.

They stepped back to admire the wall hanging. It looked perfect in their soon-to-be new sisters' bedroom.

Now the room was ready. Matching pink spreads covered the beds. Fancy pink curtains and pretty white blinds dressed up the windows.

"I like this room better than mine," Carly said.

Abby swung her sister around. "I'll trade *your* room for mine."

"Nope," Carly said.

Abby had Carly's room when she was little. There was a secret place in the closet. A secret, secret place. She missed hiding there with a flashlight and a good book.

Now Carly had the room. And the secret place.

Sometimes Abby and Carly hid there together. Abby would read softly to Carly. Mother often forgot to look for them there.

"Meet me in five seconds," Abby whispered.

"Where?" Carly said.

"In the secret place," Abby said. "We have secret plans to make."

Carly's eyes shone. "Okay!" she said, and she dashed out of the room.

Abby hoped things wouldn't change too much when her Korean sisters arrived next Saturday.

But . . . she would wait before sharing the secret place with them. Just a little while.

Two

Abby pulled a pillow into the secret place. "Shh! Don't make a sound." She slid the skinny door shut.

Abby switched on two flashlights. One for Carly. One for herself.

"Call the meeting to order," Carly whispered.

"Okay. The meeting will come to order. Now, is there any news?"

"Nope," Carly said. "Get to the important stuff. What's the secret plan?"

"Let's buy welcome-home presents for our new sisters."

"Like what?" Carly asked.

"Let's buy matching bears—bride bears!" Abby said.

"With lots of white lace." Carly wiggled all over.

Abby twirled her flashlight. "Mommy and Daddy will be surprised, too."

Carly grinned. "If we keep it a secret."

"When Daddy buys gas for the car, we'll ride along," Abby said. She planned everything. She always did.

Abby had another idea. "Let's make cards for our sisters, too."

"Out of pink paper," Carly said.

"And lace from Mommy's sewing box," Abby said.

Carly clapped her hands. "To match the bears' gowns."

The girls did their hand-over-hand secret code. Then they prayed.

"Dear Lord," Abby began, "we're getting new sisters."

"They might not know about You," Carly added.

Abby finished the prayer. "Please help us show Your love to them. In Jesus' name, amen."

They turned off the flashlights and crawled out of the closet.

Abby curled up on Carly's bed and cuddled two teddy bears.

Carly looked worried. "What about our

secret place? Can we keep it a secret from our new sisters?"

"Definitely," Abby said. "But not for *too* long."

Carly looked like she was going to cry.

"What's wrong?" Abby asked. She moved close to her sister.

"I'm afraid you won't be my best friend anymore," Carly whimpered. She hugged her bear. "Maybe you'll like our new sisters better."

"Don't be silly," Abby said, patting Carly's hair. She wished her own hair would grow long and curly like Carly's.

"Let's make a braid," Abby said.

"Goody!" Carly said. She hopped off the bed to get some hair ties.

"Make four braids," Carly begged.

"Four will look silly," Abby said.

Carly pouted. "Come on, Abby. Just for fun?"

Abby tossed the hair ties onto the bed. She stomped out of Carly's room. She could hear Carly yelling for Mother.

Let her tattle. Abby didn't care.

It would be great having a sister who wasn't such a baby.

Three

bby put the matching bride bears in a yellow basket.

"I'll carry it," Carly said.

Abby slid the welcome-home cards into the basket.

Carly twisted her hair. "Do you think they've seen bride bears before?"

"Maybe. Maybe not. There will be lots of stuff in the United States they've never seen."

"When will we give the presents?" Carly asked.

"You'll see," Abby said. She wished Carly would stop asking so many questions.

■■■

The airport buzzed with people. Some carried suitcases. Others pushed carts and pulled luggage.

Mrs. Roop, the caseworker, spotted the airline schedule. "Flight 225 is late." She pointed at the screen above their heads.

Abby and Carly groaned.

"Let's have some dessert while we wait," Mother suggested.

Mrs. Roop got special gate passes so they could meet the plane. After going through security, they strolled toward the snack shop.

"Show us the pictures again," Abby said after dessert.

Her father pulled out pictures of two Korean girls.

Carly stood on tiptoes to see the pictures. "Will they get homesick?"

"Our home will soon become their home," her father said. "We want to make things easy for them. You and Abby can help us." He hugged Carly.

"We'll help them learn our ways, Daddy," Abby said.

Carly nodded. "And God's ways. We promise."

Abby couldn't wait to give the bride bears to her new sisters.

She remembered getting her first bear dressed as a bride two years ago, at Christmas. Her father had read the Christmas story from the Bible on Christmas Eve. Everyone opened one present. They saved the rest for Christmas morning.

Abby's was a bride bear. It had a tiny red bow on its veil.

That same Christmas, Abby's parents had told them the plan to adopt Korean girls. It was a long wait. Too long for Abby. She had always wished for another sister closer to her own age. Soon she would have that sister. Carly would, too.

Abby thought the hour would never end. She leaned against her mother, who seemed tired. Maybe the waiting bothered her, too.

At last, flight 225 arrived. Abby was excited as her family waited at gate B-7. The area was full of families and caseworkers. All of them waited to welcome Korean kids to the U.S.

Abby held her breath. There were hundreds

of people. How would they find their sisters? Or Miss Lin, the escort who brought them from Korea?

This could definitely be a problem, Abby thought.

Definitely.

Four

A bby spun around. Her parents and Mrs. Roop stood behind her. "Quick! Get the pictures out." She tugged on her father's coat sleeve.

"We know what our sisters look like," Carly insisted.

But Abby wanted to be double sure.

"We'll stay here and wait for the escort," her father said. He unfolded a paper square and gave it to Abby with the pictures. On the paper were the words *HUNTER FAMILY*.

"Great idea, Daddy," Abby said, holding it high. "I'm going to explode if we don't see them soon."

"Be patient, dear," Mrs. Roop said. "It won't be much longer."

"I can't wait," Abby said. "Come on, Carly, let's go look for them." She handed the sign to her father but kept the pictures. Grabbing Carly's hand, Abby led the way through the crowd.

In the far corner sat two girls.

Abby studied the girls, then the pictures. "What do you think?" she asked Carly.

"Maybe they grew a lot."

Abby inched closer. She saw the name tag on the escort. It was not Miss Lin, but Abby felt brave. "Excuse me, do you know who Miss Lin is?"

The lady smiled. "Are you getting a new sister?"

"Two," Abby said. She felt like a jitterbug inside.

The lady pointed. "Miss Lin is over there."

"Thank you," Abby said, looking. She stood stone still. "Something's crazy wrong," she whispered.

Carly came closer. "What is?"

"Can't you see? Miss Lin is with two *boys*!"

The girls stared.

"Let's find our *sisters*," Abby said. She walked up to Miss Lin.

24

Carly followed.

Miss Lin knew nothing about sisters. She introduced the boys. "I'd like you to meet Li Sung Jin and his little brother, Li Choon Koo," she said.

Carly reached out to shake hands.

Abby turned away. She hurried to find her parents and Mrs. Roop. "Daddy! Mommy! Come quick! Something's crazy wrong!"

They pushed through the crowd and found Miss Lin again. She introduced the boys, who bowed to Abby's parents.

Mrs. Roop studied some papers. So did Miss Lin.

Abby watched her mother's face turn pale. She was puzzled at the twinkle in her father's eyes.

The Korean boys sat down and waited. They looked stiff and scared as Abby's father led Mrs. Roop around the corner.

Abby stared at the boys' dark blue-black hair. The younger boy was skinny. She couldn't see a single muscle on him.

The older boy had sad eyes. He played with a shiny round tag. He seemed to be in charge of his little brother, Choon Koo.

Abby walked around behind the seat for a better look. She was dying to see Sung Jin's silver tag.

What is it? she wondered.

Both boys sat as straight as boards.

At last, the grown-ups returned.

"Let's take a walk," Mother suggested.

The Hunter family huddled in the hallway.

"There's been a mistake," Mr. Hunter explained.

"But I . . . uh . . . we don't want brothers," Abby said.

"Your sisters will arrive in three days." He put his arms around Abby and Carly.

"What about the boys?" Carly asked.

Mother answered, "They will stay with us until Mrs. Roop clears up the mistake."

"We have to *keep* them?" Abby cried.

"It's only three days," said her father.

"Oh no!" Abby shouted. "Where will they sleep?"

"In the new room," Mother said softly.

"Not our *sisters'* room," Abby said. She pushed the presents down in the basket. She looked at Carly. "Keep the bears hidden."

"Good idea," said Carly. "But what kind of gifts can we give them?"

Father smiled. "What about kindness? That's one gift these boys could use right now."

Abby stared at the floor. "They won't want bride bears, that's for sure," she said.

Her throat felt like there was a lump in it. *This can't be happening*, she thought.

Five

Abby lagged behind as Sung Jin and Choon Koo walked between her parents down the long hallway.

Abby's father talked to them. They seemed to understand English. Choon Koo kept nodding—not talking.

Carly giggled. She pointed to a crop of hair sticking straight out on Choon Koo's head.

Abby poked her. "Shh!"

Abby stared at Sung Jin's wrinkled shorts and T-shirt. *He must have slept in them*, she thought. *Boys! How will I ever get through the next three days?*

They waited for Father to bring the car around.

Abby set down the yellow basket.

Choon Koo stared at the shiny paper peeking out. He bent down to look inside. "Pret-ty pa-per," he said slowly.

Before Abby could stop him, he pulled out a present. His brother spoke to him in Korean.

Choon Koo held the present up. He turned it over and over.

Abby wished her mother would do something.

In a flash, the wrapping paper was off! A bride bear smiled up at Choon Koo.

Abby thought she would choke.

Sung Jin grabbed the bear away from his brother. He turned it around and around, giggling.

Abby looked at Mother. "Stop them!" she cried.

Mother raised a finger to her lips.

■■■

On the ride home, Choon Koo balanced a bear bride on his feet. So did Sung Jin. Then they bounced the bears on their sandals, pointing and giggling.

The giggling bugged Abby. And the bears

would be dirty when her sisters finally came. *Phooey!*

Carly turned around in the van's middle seat. Her eyes got big.

Abby looked away. She couldn't wait to get home. "How many more minutes?" she asked her father.

"Be polite, honey," he said.

Polite. Usually that was easy. But not today! Today she would call her friend Stacy Henry. Maybe Stacy would let her move in for three days.

Besides, Stacy owed her a favor. A double dabble favor.

Last month, Abby had been covering for Stacy at recess when a stray puppy wandered onto the playground. He had looked sick and sad and needed help. Stacy had whispered her plan to Abby.

Abby talked to the playground teacher while Stacy hid the sick cockapoo under her jacket. She sneaked to the edge of the playground. Then she raced home with him, three houses away.

Later, Abby had helped Stacy talk her mother into keeping the cuddly white dog.

It was a double dabble favor.

"We're home!" shouted Carly.

The boys leaned forward to look.

Abby couldn't wait to get to the phone. *Stacy will help me*, thought Abby. *The Cul-de-Sac Kids always stick together!*

She ran into the house—away from the boys.

Six

Inside, Abby grabbed the phone. She told Stacy about the boys and the crazy mix-up.

"What will you do?" Stacy asked.

"I'll call Dunkum," Abby said. "He can teach them to shoot baskets. That could take three days." She laughed.

Carly ran into the kitchen. "The boys undressed the bride bears," she whispered in Abby's other ear.

"Yikes! Gotta go." Abby hung up the phone and hurried upstairs.

The boys' door was open. Abby stopped in the hallway. She couldn't believe what she saw.

Sung Jin was dancing with a wedding dress on his head. "Dance," he said. "Dance!"

He twirled around faster and faster. The white lace dress slid off his head.

Abby caught it. "This goes on the bears for our sisters."

Sung Jin looked around. "Sisters?" He pointed to Carly. "She is sister."

"Our *new* sisters are coming in three days." Under her breath, Abby added, "They better come."

Choon Koo came running out of the closet. He held up a girl's slip and waved the hanger around as he giggled. Then he jumped onto one of the beds. He pulled at the pink curtain.

"Be careful," Abby said. "The curtains will fall down."

"Down, down. Take them down," he chanted. "I don't like."

Sung Jin walked out of the room. Choon Koo climbed off the bed and followed his brother.

Abby held her breath. She felt all shaky inside.

Carly chased after the boys.

Abby looked down at the bedroom rug.

Something shiny was lying there. She leaned down. It was Sung Jin's round tag!

Strange marks were on each side. *This must be Korean writing,* thought Abby. She slipped the silver tag into her pocket.

Abby went to the kitchen. Mother was cooking with the new rice cooker.

Abby sniffed the air. "What's for supper?"

"Rice," Mother said. "With kimchi on the side."

Abby pinched her nose. "Smells terrible."

"The boys will like it," Mother said.

Abby groaned. "Will our sisters like it, too?"

Mother nodded.

"What's in this kimchi stuff?" Abby said.

"You'll eat better if you don't know," Mother said, smiling.

"Sounds scary. What else are we having?"

"Hot dogs, baked beans, and chips," Mother said.

"That's what I'm having." Abby ran to find Carly. She had to warn her not to eat the Korean food. It smelled rotten.

Carly was outside on the driveway with the boys. The Cul-de-Sac Kids were there, too.

Dunkum dribbled his basketball. He showed off his fancy moves.

Jason Birchall chased behind Dunkum, trying to grab the ball. He was hyper, as always.

Stacy Henry showed off her puppy. Carly played with his floppy ears.

Dee Dee Winters sneaked a suck on her thumb.

Eric Hagel showed up on his cool ten-speed. "What's up?"

"Let's have a meeting," Abby said.

Dunkum shot another basket. "Right now?"

Carly squealed, "Wow! Nine in a row!"

"Let's get acquainted with the new boys on the block," said Stacy.

Sung Jin and Choon Koo turned toward each other. Choon Koo reached for his big brother.

Abby felt sad. She wondered how it felt being stuck with a family who didn't want boys.

Then she dug into her jeans pocket and handed the silver tag to Sung Jin. His sad eyes lit up.

"This must've fallen when you danced," she said.

Sung Jin held it tightly. "Thank you," he said.

Then Abby had an idea. A double dabble good idea.

Seven

Abby called the kids over to the porch. "Let's help Sung Jin and Choon Koo get to know us. Everyone tell your name and how old you are," she said.

"And your pig-out foods," yelled Jason Birchall.

The kids laughed as they sat on the porch.

"Leave it to Abby," Eric said. He put the kickstand down on his bike.

"I'll go first," Dunkum offered.

The kids stretched their necks to look up when Dunkum stood.

Choon Koo said, "Very tall boy."

Dunkum told his name. "I'm a third-grade health nut. I eat salads with alfalfa sprouts and tomatoes."

"Yuck!" Carly squealed, holding her nose.

Dunkum stretched his arms. "They make me grow tall. Tall enough to dunk the ball. Well, almost."

The kids cheered.

"Who's next?" Abby asked.

"I am." Carly said her name with Anne in the middle. "I'm in first grade, and I'm starting to dream about rice." She grinned at Choon Koo. He laughed his high giggle.

Sung Jin sat straight and still. "I am Li Sung Jin, age eight. I like American rice."

Choon Koo jumped up. "I like Jimmy name." He patted his chest. "I now am Jimmy. Jimmy eat and eat rice."

Abby couldn't believe it. Choon Koo *looked* like a Jimmy. "Jimmy," she said, pointing to him. "Pick someone."

He pointed to Stacy Henry, who held up her puppy. "I'm Stacy, and this is Sunday Funnies. He finds the funnies in the Sunday newspaper before anyone else."

Dee Dee giggled.

Stacy continued. "I'm in third grade. I like pizza the best. We only have it on weekends."

Abby pointed to Dee Dee. "Your turn," she said.

"I'm Dee Dee Winters." She wiped off her wet thumb. "I'm in first grade, and chocolate ice cream is my favorite. I don't know why. It just is." Dee Dee sat down and looked at Eric.

"Hi, I'm Eric Hagel. We moved here from Germany two years ago. I'm in Abby's class, third grade." He paused and smiled at her. "I eat SweeTarts. My grandpa has pockets full of them. He's the watchmaker up the street." Eric sat down beside Dunkum.

"SweeTarts aren't real food," Abby teased.

"Are so," Eric said. He threw her one.

She caught it.

"Where's mine?" Jason asked.

"You're not supposed to have sugar," Eric said. "Remember?"

Jason crossed his eyes. "My name's Jason Allen Birchall. But my friends call me Jason."

Dee Dee giggled. "Nice name."

"Now it's *your* turn," Eric told Abby.

She stood up. "Abby Hunter. Third grade. My favorite food is spaghetti. It slides down when I slurp it."

"Hurrah for spaghetti!" cheered Jason.

"Don't forget the grated cheese," yelled Dee Dee.

Then Abby said, "Sung Jin and Choon Koo will be here for only three days."

Choon Koo stood up. "Not Choon Koo. I *Jimmy.*"

Sung Jin pulled his brother back down.

"I forgot about your new name," Abby said. "I'm sorry." She really was.

"The kids on Blossom Hill Lane stick together no matter how long they stay," said Eric. "Welcome to our cul-de-sac."

Suddenly, Sung Jin's eyes sparkled. The sadness was gone.

Abby's mother called for supper. Sung Jin and Jimmy hurried inside.

Jason started to invite himself, but then he smelled the kimchi. He held his nose instead. "Are we having a meeting next week?"

"When our Korean sisters come," Abby said.

She hoped it was soon. Very soon.

Eight

I t was Monday morning.

Sung Jin and Jimmy sat on the porch swing ready for a visit to Blossom Hill School. They wore new American clothes.

Abby tied a double knot in her sneakers. One red. One blue.

Carly ran out of the house.

Abby led the way down the cul-de-sac. The other kids came dashing out. At the corner, they bunched together to cross the street.

When they reached the school yard, Abby shouted, "Countdown to recess!"

"Recess, recess," the kids chanted. Then they scattered in different directions.

Jimmy followed Carly and Dee Dee to first grade.

Sung Jin went with Abby and Stacy to third. Jason darted ahead of Eric and Dunkum.

In math, Sung Jin tried the problems. He had trouble, so the teacher gave him an easier paper. Kids bumped into one another trying to help him.

At recess, Jason saved a swing for Sung Jin. Eric asked him to play soccer. Dunkum got dibs on lunch.

Abby and Stacy hung from the bars.

"Still want to move in?" Stacy asked.

"Guess not. Our sisters will be coming soon."

"What will happen to Jimmy and Sung Jin?" Stacy asked.

"I don't know. They're leaving with Mrs. Roop soon."

Abby hoped the boys would like their new family.

■ ■ ■

On the way home, Abby skipped over the sidewalk cracks.

The cul-de-sac boys yelled for Sung Jin and Jimmy to play basketball.

Carly went to Dee Dee's house.

Abby walked home alone.

In the house, Mother was cooking rice again.

Abby hurried to the secret place. Tomorrow would be the best day. Her sisters were coming!

She flipped on the flashlight and slid the narrow door shut. Finding her Sunday school paper, she read the story. It was about secret sins.

She looked up Psalm 19:12 in her Bible. *No one can see all his own mistakes. Forgive me for my secret sins.*

Abby felt funny inside. *How many secret sins do I have?* she wondered. She talked to God about it.

Later, Abby heard her parents talking. She crawled out of the closet to listen.

Mother sounded upset. "Mrs. Roop called this morning. She wants us to keep the boys another week."

"How do you feel about it, dear?" Abby's father asked.

"I really don't know," Mother said. "The longer they stay, the harder it will be for them to leave."

Father chuckled. "They are having a great time, aren't they?"

"A great time tearing the bedroom apart," Mother said.

"It's not much of a boys' bedroom, now, is it, dear?"

Is Daddy sticking up for them? Abby wondered.

Mother's voice shook. "Where are the girls? *Our girls?*"

Abby held her breath.

"Mrs. Roop is handling that," her father said. "Let's trust the Lord to take care of things."

Screech! Outside, a car slammed on its brakes.

Abby ran to the window. She saw Sunday Funnies limp away from the car and hide under Eric's porch.

Sung Jin chased the hurt puppy. He crawled under the porch and coaxed the puppy out. Then he took off his jacket.

Eric and Dunkum came running. Gently, they lifted the puppy into Sung Jin's jacket.

Abby dashed downstairs. "Mommy, come quick!" she called. "It's Sung, er . . . I mean, it's Sunday Funnies."

Mother hurried outside to Sung Jin. "Are you all right?"

Sung Jin looked bashful, but he nodded.

"Sung's fine," Jason called from across the street. "Stacy's puppy's hurt."

The boys made a three-cornered stretcher with Sung's jacket. Slowly, step by step, they carried the cockapoo across the street.

Stacy stroked Sunday Funnies as the driver got out of the car. His face was white. He looked at the dog and patted his head.

The boys carried Sunday Funnies to Abby's mother. Stacy followed close behind.

"I'll call the vet," Mrs. Hunter said. She hurried inside the house.

Stacy followed. Abby held her hand.

Soon the kitchen was filled with droopy-faced kids.

Sung Jin and Eric and Dunkum laid Sunday Funnies on the floor. They knelt around him. Abby thought Stacy was praying.

Abby's mother talked to the vet.

Carly came into the house. "What happened?"

"Sunday Funnies got hit by a car," Abby said.

"Oh no!" she cried, sitting on the floor near the puppy.

Mother hung up the phone. "The vet wants to check him for broken bones."

"I'll call my mom at work," Stacy said. "She'll drive us to the vet. Thank you, Mrs. Hunter." Then she turned to Sung Jin. "Thank *you*. I'm going to miss you when you leave tomorrow."

After the kids were gone, Abby whispered to Carly, "Meet me in the secret place."

Inside the secret place, Abby told Carly about the boys staying longer.

"Another week?" said Carly. "Will we ever get our sisters?"

"I guess so," Abby said. "I hope so . . . I think."

Nine

The next day, Abby jumped a pretend hopscotch while she waited for Stacy. At last, Stacy skipped down her front steps.

"Hi," Abby said. "How's Sunday Funnies?"

"Limping."

Abby kicked a stone down the sidewalk. "Lucky he didn't get killed."

"Poor thing," Stacy said. "I sneaked some waffles to help cheer him up. What did you have for breakfast?"

"Rice."

"Cream of rice?"

Abby sighed. "No, rice rice."

"You're kidding."

Abby laughed. "It's not so bad."

Stacy grinned. "How are the boys doing?"

"Sung Jin and Jimmy are learning to thank God for their food," Abby said. "And Sung Jin keeps reminding God that he's eating *American* rice now."

"Do the boys know about Jesus?" asked Stacy.

"We teach them something new every day from the Bible. They'll have a good idea by the time they leave."

"What if they don't get a Christian family?" Stacy asked.

Abby hadn't thought of that. "I will pray that they do!"

"Will Sung Jin always have two names?" Stacy asked.

Abby hopped on one foot. "Only till he chooses an English name," she said.

■■■

After school, it was snowing fast. Abby scuffed her shoes on the snowy sidewalk.

Mother looked up from her Korean cookbook as Abby came into the kitchen.

"Is Carly home yet?" Abby asked.

"They were just here," her mother said.

"They?"

"Carly and Choon Koo."

"You mean Jimmy."

Mother closed the cookbook. "Who?"

"Choon Koo is Jimmy now."

"He can't pick his name," Mother said.

"But he *wants* to be called Jimmy."

"His parents will choose his name," her mother insisted.

Abby didn't like that. Choon Koo was Jimmy. He even looked like a Jimmy!

Abby peeked in Carly's room. No one there. She looked in the boys' room. "Oh no!" she wailed.

The pink bedspreads were rolled up and stuffed under the beds. The corners were sticking out.

The bride bears stood side by side on the bookcase. They looked like boy bears now. Each had a red paper hat stuck to its head.

Scissors and leftover scraps lay on the floor.

Dresser drawers hung open. Mother's pink wall hanging lay folded inside the bottom drawer.

Those horrible boys!

She turned to go, calling for Carly.

No answer.

She dashed to the secret place and slid open the narrow door.

There sat Carly reading to Jimmy.

"What are you doing?" Abby shouted.

"Helping Jimmy read," Carly said, shining the flashlight in Abby's face.

Abby frowned at her little sister. *Carly knows better. Jimmy doesn't belong in here!*

Abby churned with anger. She ran through the snow to Dunkum's next door to help him with his spelling.

Phooey! Carly had shared the secret place with Jimmy. Things were crazy wrong.

Ten

Later, Abby ran back home. She dashed to her sister's room. "How could you?"

"What?" Carly asked.

"You showed Jimmy our secret place!" Abby hollered.

"So what?"

Abby stared at Carly. "You didn't tell him our secret code, did you?"

Carly frowned. "What's *wrong* with you, Abby?"

"Nothing."

Carly lined up her stuffed animals in a row on her bed. "Abby, why don't you like Jimmy and Sung Jin?"

Abby held her breath. "They aren't sisters," Abby said slowly. "That's why."

■■■

Wednesday at breakfast, Mother said, "Come home right after school. All bedrooms must be cleaned."

"Mine *is* clean," Carly said.

"Spotless?" Mother asked.

Carly nodded.

"What's the hurry?" Abby asked.

"Mrs. Roop is coming after supper," Mother said.

"What for?" Carly asked.

"For a visit," Mother said. She wiped the table.

"To check our rooms?" Carly asked.

Abby wished Carly would stop asking questions. She felt all jumpy again. Mother knew more than she was telling. Abby was sure of it.

Abby followed her mother downstairs. "It's about keeping the boys, isn't it?"

Mother sat on the sofa. She patted the pillow beside her. "How do you feel about that?"

Abby's brain was in a whirl. She felt all mixed up. "I like Jimmy and Sung Jin—it's not that. I just had my hopes set on getting girls."

"I know, honey. So did I." Mother hugged Abby close. "Let's pray about it, okay?"

Abby nodded.

Later, she walked to school by herself. It was a good time to talk to God alone.

■ ■ ■

After supper, Mrs. Roop sat in the living room with Abby's parents. They talked for a long time.

Mrs. Roop visited Abby's room first. She closed the door and sat on the bed. She smelled like roses. "I like your green and yellow wallpaper. It's lovely."

Abby felt like a jitterbug.

Mrs. Roop asked questions about Sung Jin and Choon Koo.

"Choon Koo is Jimmy now," Abby said. *Why doesn't anyone pay attention?*

Mrs. Roop asked more questions. They made Abby even more jittery. "How would you like Sung Jin and Choon Koo . . . uh, Jimmy to be your brothers?"

"What about our sisters?" Abby asked.

"We've located them," she said. "The girls are still in Korea. Your parents will have to file papers again." She paused. "But the *boys* are happy here."

It sounded like a question without a question mark.

Abby wished she was alone in the secret place. She couldn't wait for Mrs. Roop to leave.

■■■

Bath time. Jimmy was yelling. Ever since his first night in this country, Jimmy had hated baths. Father gave him one anyway. Jimmy squealed louder and louder.

Maybe he's scared, thought Abby. She searched for her old plastic duck. She found it in a shoe box in her closet. Knocking on the bathroom door, Abby showed the duck to her father. "Will this help?"

Quickly, the squealing stopped.

After his bath, Jimmy brought the dripping duck to Abby.

"Keep it. It's yours," she said.

Jimmy hugged the duck.

Abby wanted to hug him, but she didn't.

Later, Sung Jin asked Abby if they could visit Stacy's puppy.

"We'll go after school tomorrow," Abby promised.

Sung Jin was grinning. *Really* grinning.

Abby wondered what it would be like having Sung Jin for a brother. But at bedtime, she prayed for her *sisters* in Korea.

Eleven

School's out for Thanksgiving!" shouted Abby on the way to Stacy's house. She rang the doorbell. Sung Jin waited beside her on the snowy porch.

Soon the door swung wide. Stacy was carrying Sunday Funnies. The little splint on his leg looked like a toy.

Sung Jin stroked the puppy. "Better?"

"He's *much* better," Stacy said. "Thanks."

"I had puppy long, long time," Sung Jin said.

"In Korea?" Stacy asked.

"Before orphanage." Sung Jin's eyes looked sad again. "My puppy look like this."

Abby felt sorry for Sung Jin. Everything he loved was in Korea.

He pulled out the shiny round tag. "I keep this."

Abby saw the Korean marks on it. "What does it mean?"

"*Haeng-bok.* In English, puppy name mean happy."

Stacy smiled. "A lot like Sunday Funnies. Good times, happy times."

Sung Jin giggled. The giggling didn't bother Abby today. She was glad to see Sung Jin having a good time. They played with Sunday Funnies until it was time for supper.

Later, after dishes were done, Abby sneaked to her father's study. She tapped on the door.

Abby held her breath. "I've decided something, Daddy."

"What is it, Abby?" He leaned back in his chair.

"I hope we can adopt Sung Jin and Jimmy." Abby's eyes filled with happy tears.

"Bless your heart," her father said. He stood up and kissed Abby's cheek.

"And . . . I have an idea," said Abby.

Her father grinned. "What is it?"

"A double dabble Thanksgiving surprise!"

"It is?" he said, playing along.

So it was settled. Tomorrow, Sung Jin and Jimmy would have a big surprise!

■■■

Early Thanksgiving morning, Abby helped Mother shine silver—knives, forks, and spoons. She set out bowls for the boys' kimchi and rice, and plates for the turkey.

Sung Jin helped Abby with the decorations—pilgrim boys and girls. A pair for each end of the table.

He pointed to the pilgrims. "Who?"

"They're pilgrims. They came to America long ago. They wanted freedom to worship God."

Sung Jin looked puzzled. "Worship?"

Abby understood. Sung Jin had never heard the story of the first Thanksgiving.

She drew a picture of pilgrims sailing the ocean in a big boat. "God kept the pilgrims safe when they came," she said. She made the waves swish around her boat.

"After a long winter, the pilgrims had a feast. They shared food with their new friends." Abby drew a long table with stick figures sitting with folded hands. "Here's how they worshipped God on the first Thanksgiving. They said thank-you in a prayer."

Sung Jin's eyes grew wide. "I learn new things here."

"I'm learning new things, too," Abby said. *About me*, she thought.

Mother came over to the table and looked at the drawings.

Sung Jin touched the pilgrim girl. "Abby best sister. She tell first Thanksgiving story."

Abby felt warm inside.

Carly and Jimmy came in just then.

"The Cul-de-Sac Kids are outside. They want to see Jimmy and Sung," Carly said.

Abby and Sung put on their jackets and hurried outdoors.

Dunkum bounced his ball on the snow-packed porch. Jason slid around trying to steal the ball.

Stacy stomped the snow off her feet. Sunday Funnies limped on his splint. Stacy picked him up and cuddled him.

Eric pulled Dee Dee on his sled. "Happy turkey day," he called.

Sung turned to look at Abby. There was a question in his dark eyes. "Turkey day?"

"Some people call it that because we eat turkey," Abby explained. "But the most important thing is to give thanks to God."

Eric pulled the sled up the driveway. He handed a bag of SweeTarts to Abby. "These are from my grandpa, for after dinner."

"Where's mine?" Jason asked, licking his lips.

"No snitching!" Dee Dee hollered.

Jason groaned and rolled his eyes.

Dee Dee's nose wrinkled up at him.

Mother peeked out just then. "Family meeting time."

"Goody!" Carly shouted.

Abby hoped the meeting was about adopting the boys. She couldn't wait to give them her big surprise!

Twelve

Abby sat next to her father in the living room.

"Something important has happened," he began. "We are going to adopt Sung Jin and Choon Koo."

Abby clapped her hands. "Yippee!" she shouted.

Jimmy and Carly jumped up and down.

"We stay here?" Sung Jin asked.

"You certainly do," Father said. "We are very proud to adopt such fine boys."

Abby glanced at her mother. She was smiling, too.

"Sung Jin needs an English name," Mother said, holding the family Bible. "We like the name Shawn."

Abby did, too. It sounded something like Sung.

Sung Jin smiled, and Mother wrote his new name in the Bible.

Jimmy leaped off his chair. "I am Jimmy. Yes?"

Mother laughed.

Father set Jimmy on his knee. "You are Jimmy Hunter."

Abby couldn't imagine any other name for him. She also couldn't imagine having more sisters instead of brothers. Not now.

"Pink comes down," Jimmy said.

Father looked puzzled. "What does he mean?"

Abby knew. "He means the pink curtains on their bedroom windows."

"Yes," said Jimmy. "All girl things come down."

Mother nodded. "All the pink and frills must go. You and Sung, er . . . Shawn can help us change your room to look like a boys' room."

Jimmy danced a jig.

Shawn tossed his silver dog tag in the air. "Yes!"

66

Abby went to get the camera. Her father took pictures of all the kids.

"There's a surprise for you," Abby whispered to Shawn.

"Surprise?" Shawn's dark eyes sparkled.

"After dinner."

At the table, Father said to join hands. Everyone bowed heads for a Thanksgiving prayer.

After the amen, Shawn spoke up. "I say thank you to God for new family. Big thank you."

Abby smiled at him across the table.

When dinner was over, Abby met her father in his study. "Are we ready for the you-know-what?"

He hugged her. "It's just the right time."

Abby called Shawn. She led him to Carly's room. She slid the narrow door open to the secret place and held her breath.

There was a fluffy puppy wagging its flouncy tail!

Shawn's eyes shone. He sat on the floor, and the puppy jumped all over him. He laughed so hard he fell backward. The puppy stood on his chest and licked his face.

Carly and Jimmy came running. The puppy yipped at them.

"Goody!" said Carly. "Is she ours?"

"We adopted her," said Abby. "But mostly, she's Shawn's."

"A good surprise," said Shawn, giggling.

"I can think of two more good surprises." First Abby looked at Jimmy, then at Shawn. "A double dabble surprise," she said.

BOOK 2

The Chicken Pox Panic

To my very own
cul-de-sac kids,
Julie, Janie,
and
Jonathan.

One

It was an itchy-gitchy Friday.

Abby Hunter sat up in bed. She rubbed the spots on her arm. On her face. And behind her knees under her pajamas.

"I hate chicken pox," she said.

"Here," said her little sister, Carly. "Put this gooey stuff on."

She gave the bottle of pink liquid to Abby. Frowning at the spots, Carly backed away.

Abby shook the bottle and turned the lid. She wrinkled her nose. The spots on her nose wiggled. "Pee-yew. It stinks."

Slowly, one at a time, Abby dabbed pink goo on her spots.

It was supposed to make the itching stop.

Abby counted to ten, waiting for the pink

goo to work. "Nothing's happening," she complained.

Carly leaned against the door. "I hope I don't get your chicken pox."

Abby dabbed another coating of goo on the bumps she could reach. "Mommy wants you to catch them," she said.

"How come?" Carly demanded.

"So you won't get them when you're grown up."

Abby put on her mint green bathrobe. She felt cozy inside, spots and all.

Carly stared at Abby. Then she pointed. "Look, Abby! You even have them on your feet."

"I know," Abby said. "I have them everywhere!"

"What do they feel like?" Carly asked.

"Ever have a giant mosquito bite?"

Carly nodded.

"Just multiply that times one hundred," Abby said.

Carly shivered and turned the doorknob. "I'm getting out of here."

"You'll be sorry if you don't get them now," Abby said. She scratched between her toes.

"Will not," Carly said.

"Will so," Abby said.

"Will not," Carly said.

"Will . . ." Abby stopped.

Mother stood in the hallway carrying a large atlas. She gave it to Abby. "Is this what you need?"

Abby reached for the book of maps. "Thanks! This is double dabble good!"

She flipped the pages to the back of the atlas. "What's the capital of South Korea?"

"Seoul," said Mother, smoothing Abby's quilt.

Carly giggled. "That's a funny name."

Abby held the book open. "You just think it is. Come see how it's spelled."

"Not me," Carly said, hugging the door. "I'm staying right here."

Abby rolled her eyes. "Afraid of my chicken pox?"

Mother gave both girls a kiss. "It's not so bad having them when you are little," she said.

"That's what I told her," said Abby.

Mother grinned and left the room.

Abby turned to page 45 in the atlas. She

leaned on her elbows, looking at the map of South Korea. With her finger, she traced the borders.

"What are you doing?" Carly asked.

"It's a secret," said Abby.

Out of the corner of her eye, she saw Carly sneaking closer.

Whoosh! Abby plopped her pillow down on top of South Korea.

TWO

Abby climbed out of bed. She went to her desk to find a ruler.

But she kept her eyes on the pillow. The one hiding page 45 in the atlas.

It was time to measure South Korea. She sat on the edge of the bed. She held the pillow over the map so Carly couldn't see.

Carly yelled, "You can't fool me. It's your homework!"

"Guess again," Abby said. She put the ruler down.

Carly stomped her foot. "Tell me this minute!"

Abby looked up from the map. "Don't be so bossy."

"Ple-e-ease, Abby?" Carly begged.

Abby looked into her sister's blue eyes. Could she trust her? "Do you promise not to tell?"

Carly grinned. "Cross my heart and hope to—"

"Don't say that," Abby said. "It's silly."

"That's how you make a promise," Carly said.

"Maybe in first grade, but not in third." Abby picked up the pillow and uncovered the map.

Carly inched closer. "What's the map for?"

Abby scratched her nose. "Shawn used to live in Korea when his name was Li Sung Jin," she said.

"I know—before we adopted him and Jimmy."

Abby leaned on the atlas. "When Shawn and Jimmy came to live in the United States, they had to leave their country behind."

"I know that," said Carly. She played with her curls. "So what's the map for?"

"It's a double dabble surprise for Shawn's ninth birthday. He's going to have the best birthday cake ever!" Abby slammed the map book shut.

"I don't get it," Carly said. "Why are you looking at maps and talking about cakes?"

Abby smiled. "Just because."

She felt like a jitterbug inside. Birthday secrets always did that.

Carly tiptoed closer. Now she stood beside Abby's bed. "Please tell me." Carly crossed her heart.

"OK, OK. Here's my secret," said Abby. "I'm going to make a cake in the shape of South Korea for Shawn's party."

Carly jumped up and down. "Goody!"

"Remember, you can't tell anyone," said Abby. "The secret could get back to Shawn."

"And that would be terrible," said Carly. But she had a silly look on her face.

"You better not tell," Abby said. She slid under the covers.

"Or what?"

"Or you'll be sorry," Abby said. She pulled up the quilt. "I feel lousy."

"Chicken pox does that. Mommy said so." Carly opened the door to leave.

Abby was glad. She was tired of Carly's chatter. And all that silly cross-your-heart stuff.

She hid the atlas under her bed.

Then she fell asleep wishing she hadn't told anyone about the cake.

Three

bby woke up when Carly brought in a supper tray. On it was chicken soup and honey toast.

Stacy Henry came for a visit. She was Abby's best friend.

Stacy pulled a get-well card out of her pocket.

"Here. I made this for you in art today." She gave it to Abby.

Abby read the card. It was a silly sad face with spots all over. It was Abby's itchy-gitchy chicken pox face.

At the bottom of the card was a happy face—*after* the chicken pox.

"Hope you get well quick," Stacy said. She untied her sneakers and pulled them off.

"Thanks," Abby said. "I have to. My brother's birthday is in two weeks."

"And Abby's going to bake him a cake," Carly said.

Abby stared at Carly. *She better not tell!*

Carly put her hand over her mouth. "Oops, I mean, Abby's going to—"

"Just be quiet," Abby warned.

Abby wanted to take back the secret. Phooey, little sisters—what a pain!

Carly's friend, Dee Dee Winters, sneaked into the bedroom just then. She giggled when she saw Abby. "I brought you something, Abby-pox."

She gave Abby a plastic ring.

"Thanks," Abby said, sliding it on her pinky.

Carly stood beside the bed. "Wanna see Abby's spots?" She pulled back the covers.

Dee Dee's eyes got big.

"Come look," Abby said. She propped her pillows up behind her, showing off the bumps.

"They're everywhere!" Dee Dee said.

Abby leaned against her pillows and grinned. "They kept me out of school all week."

Stacy sat on the edge of the bed.

"Look out or you'll catch them!" Carly shouted, pulling on Stacy's arm.

Stacy smiled. "It's OK. I had them last year."

Carly frowned. "You might get them again."

"Mother says you only get them once," Stacy said.

"Really?" said Carly.

Dee Dee crept toward the bed. "That's why I came over. My mother wants me to catch them." She held her breath like she was scared, but then she sat down on the bed.

"We could get them together," said Carly.

Dee Dee jumped up and said good-bye. She ran out of the room, and Carly raced after her.

Abby slipped back under her quilt. "Quick, close the door," she said to Stacy.

Stacy hurried to shut the door. "Good idea. We have to talk."

"What's up?" asked Abby.

"Promise you won't tell?"

Abby sat straight up in bed. A secret!

"Well, *do* you?" Stacy unzipped the pocket on her jacket. She pulled out a piece of paper.

Abby nodded. "I promise."

She felt like a jitterbug for sure.

Four

Abby looked at Stacy's paper.

There was a tree with a bunch of branches and lines on it.

Stacy pointed to the paper. "Do you know what this is?"

Abby saw the names on the lines. "A family tree?"

Stacy nodded. "It's for school."

"Wish I could go back soon," said Abby. "Looks like fun."

"Not really," said Stacy.

"How come?"

"I asked my mother, and she didn't know very many names," Stacy said sadly.

There were lots of blank lines in the branches on Stacy's paper.

Just then, someone knocked on the door.

"Shh!" said Stacy. She stuffed the paper into her pocket. "Don't say a word about this."

Abby nodded. Then she called, "Who is it?"

"Shawn" came the voice through the door. "Is Snow White in there?"

"Come look for your dog if you want," Abby said.

The door opened. In came Shawn waving a dog collar. "Snow White gone."

"Are you sure?" Abby said.

"Carly say, 'Time for Snow White to get chicken pox.'" Shawn looked worried.

Abby and Stacy giggled.

Shawn looked puzzled. "Dogs get pox?"

Abby smiled. "Definitely not."

"Good," said Shawn, smiling now.

"Maybe Jimmy took Snow White for a walk. Look for him, and you might find your dog," Abby suggested.

Shawn held up the dog collar. "Take dog walking without leash? Not smart."

"You're right," Abby said. She thought about Snow White's favorite place. "Look in the secret place, behind Carly's closet," she said. "Snow White likes to sleep there."

"Good thinking," Shawn said. He turned to

Stacy. "Stay there. Do not leave soon." Then he ran out of the room.

Stacy looked surprised. "I wonder what he wants."

Abby said, "Quick! Show me your family tree again."

Stacy unfolded the paper. "Hurry, I don't want Shawn . . . uh, or anyone to see."

"Why not?" Abby asked.

"Because I think I'm adopted." Stacy looked like she was going to cry.

"You do?" Abby said, surprised.

Stacy played with the zipper on her jacket. "My mother can't find my baby pictures. Not a single one."

Abby scratched the bumps on her feet. "Maybe they got lost when you moved here."

"That was a long time ago," Stacy said.

"Wait a minute!" Abby said. "You can't be adopted. Everyone says your eyes look just like your dad's."

"That's what my mother says. But I don't remember him. He moved out years ago."

Abby took a deep breath. She wished Stacy's father lived at home. Right here on Blossom Hill Lane—the best cul-de-sac ever!

"I have an idea," said Abby. "Look at your birth certificate. It will tell you the truth."

"I tried that," Stacy said. "My mother can't find it, either."

Abby frowned. "Is it lost?"

"I told you—I must be adopted," Stacy said. "Just like your Korean brothers and Snow White and . . ." She stopped.

Abby threw the covers off and scooted across the bed. She put her arm around Stacy. "And what?"

"And if it's true, I don't even know where I came from."

Abby grabbed a Kleenex box off her dresser. "Here, wipe your eyes," she said. "Why don't you ask your mother?"

Stacy shook her head. "I did. She's too busy."

Now Abby was *really* worried.

Something was going on. She had to find out exactly what.

And fast!

Five

Someone pounded on Abby's bedroom door.
"Who's there?" Stacy called.

"Snow White and Goliath," said a tiny voice.

Abby giggled. "That must be my little brother."

Stacy tossed her family tree paper under the bed.

Sure enough, Jimmy came in carrying a fluffy white puppy. "Snow White sleeping in secret place. Waiting for kiss from Goliath . . . to wake up," he said.

Abby and Stacy giggled.

"You have a fairy tale mixed in with a Bible story," Abby said. "Snow White is *not* in the Bible."

"And Goliath would never kiss a puppy," said Stacy.

"Jimmy's still learning about the Bible," Abby said. She liked telling her adopted brothers the story of David and Goliath. In Korea, they had only heard Bible stories in the orphanage. Nowhere else.

Jimmy grinned and put down the puppy. Snow White hopped up on the bed and licked Abby's face.

"No, no, Snow White," shouted Jimmy. "Must not get itchy pox."

Just then, Shawn came in with his school notebook.

Snow White leaped up on him, too.

"You are here!" said Shawn, petting his puppy. He put the collar on Snow White.

Then he showed his notebook to Stacy. He opened it to his family tree. He pointed to the grandfather line. "What did teacher say if person die?" he asked Stacy.

"You still write his name. Then the year he was born and the year he died, if you know it," Stacy said.

"Oh," Shawn said. "I do not know when grandfather die. Mother in Korea not tell me."

Abby scratched her neck. "Let's see your family tree," she said to Shawn.

There were two names on each line. One for his Korean birth parents and one for Abby's parents.

Shawn's eyes shone. "I have two families now."

Stacy peeked at Shawn's family tree. She pointed to the line on the left side. "Is this your birth mother's name?"

Shawn smiled. "Yes. First mother live in Korea. She very sick. Mrs. Hunter, Abby's mother, now my mother. We very lucky she adopt Jimmy and me."

Stacy thought for a moment. "I think you're lucky, too."

Abby handed the notebook back. "Your writing is getting better, Shawn. I think it's an A+ paper."

Shawn's eyes lit up. "Good. I think, too."

Then he and Jimmy left the room.

Stacy sat on the rug, beside the bed. "I want to know if I'm adopted," she said.

"I'm good at solving mysteries," said Abby. "I'll help you."

"When can we start?" Stacy asked.

"As soon as my bumps crust over," said Abby.

Stacy leaned down and looked under the bed.

"What are you doing?" Abby said, remembering the atlas she hid there. She held her breath.

"Finding my family tree," said Stacy. "I hid it under here." She pulled out the book of maps. "Hey, what's this?"

Abby's heart beat fast. "A project I have." She wished Stacy wouldn't ask.

"For school?" Stacy asked.

"Uh . . . no," said Abby, not wanting to tell.

"What for?"

Abby scratched her head. "I can't say." She pulled her knees up to her chin, thinking. About the most creative birthday cake in the world!

"Come on, Abby. I can keep a secret," Stacy said.

"I know."

"Then tell me, or I'll have to solve your mystery, too. I'll call it the Mystery of the Map Book," Stacy said.

But Abby wasn't worried. Not one bit. Stacy couldn't solve a mystery even if she tried.

Six

It was Wednesday.

Abby's bumps were scabby, so she went back to school.

At recess, Stacy and Abby met near the swings.

"I have a plan," Abby said.

Stacy looked around to see if anyone was listening. "About my adoption?" she whispered.

Abby nodded. "When does your mother get home?"

"5:30."

"That gives us plenty of time. Today, I'll solve your mystery," Abby said.

Stacy cheered, "All right! Meet me at my house after school."

When the bell rang after school, both girls raced toward Blossom Hill Lane. The wind was blowing hard.

Abby dug her hands into her coat pockets. A quarter was in one pocket. Three gummy bears were in the other.

The cul-de-sac seemed quiet as they entered Stacy's house. Sunday Funnies, Stacy's cockapoo, barked as they came in the door. He shook his furry white head.

The girls headed straight for the master bedroom.

Stacy pointed to a file drawer. "My mother keeps important papers in there," she said.

Abby's heart pounded. She felt like a jitterbug inside. *This isn't right,* Abby worried. *We shouldn't be snooping.*

Then Abby looked at Stacy's face. This was something important, and she wanted to help her friend.

Abby took a deep breath and pulled the handle.

Locked!

"Where's the key?" she asked.

"I don't know," said Stacy.

"Let's look around." Abby led the way.

First, to the closet. They looked in the shoe boxes. No key.

They looked in the lamp table beside the bed. A package of gum, some tissues, and a Bible were inside. But no key.

"Where could it be?" asked Abby. "Think hard."

Stacy scratched her head. "Where would *you* hide a key?"

"Good question!" Abby dashed off to the kitchen.

"Now what?" asked Stacy.

Abby went to the refrigerator. She opened the freezer door. "This is the safest place in the house," Abby said. "In case of fire, the freezer is a good place to keep important stuff." She pulled out three pizza boxes.

Stacy took out a half gallon of ice cream. And bags of strawberries from her grandma's garden. There were frozen vegetables. A pot roast. Two packages of hot dogs. The girls stacked them on the floor.

Sunday Funnies sniffed at the carton of ice cream.

Abby peeked in the freezer. "Well, that's it. There's nothing left."

Then she spotted something shiny way in the back.

It was a key stuck to the side.

"Look at this!" shouted Abby, grabbing the key.

"You're amazing!" Stacy said as the girls raced back to the bedroom.

Abby turned the lock and opened the file drawer. "Look under the B's for birth certificate," she said.

Stacy found the file folder and pulled it out.

Opening the folder, Abby saw only one birth certificate. It was Stacy's mother's.

"See what I mean?" said Stacy.

Abby thought for a minute. *Maybe Stacy is right. Maybe she is adopted!*

Detectives don't cry. But Abby sure felt like it when she saw Stacy's face. Being adopted was a *good* thing. Why hadn't Stacy's mother told her?

Then she remembered the freezer. And all the food. "Hurry, before your mom gets home!"

The girls raced to the kitchen.

"Oh no!" cried Stacy. "I'm in trouble now."

Sunday Funnies was crouched under the

table. He had torn the pot roast open and was half finished with the ice cream. Ice cream was all over his face and paws.

"Quick! We have to do something fast!"

Abby took the ice cream carton away from Sunday Funnies. She threw it in the trash along with the slobbery pot roast.

The girls piled the rest of the food back into the freezer.

Then Stacy cleaned up the floor.

"I'll use my allowance to buy another roast. And some ice cream," Abby said. Then she remembered Shawn's birthday surprise. Buying ice cream and a pot roast would use up all her savings.

Phooey! So much for the greatest cake in the world, she thought.

Abby hurried home to get her money, a huge lump in her throat.

Seven

It was starting to snow.

Abby hopped on her bike and headed for the grocery store. Snowflakes tickled her face.

She pedaled hard, thinking about the cake that could have been.

Now Shawn would never get his birthday cake. All because of the silly detective stuff! *I should never have sneaked around.*

At the store, Abby found a roast. It looked like the one Sunday Funnies had torn open. She found the same brand of ice cream. She paid for it with every cent she had.

Pushing sad thoughts away, she headed for Stacy's. At last, she rang the doorbell.

"Come in!" called Stacy. "I'm in the bathroom giving my dog a bath. He's a terrible mess."

"I have another pot roast and some ice cream," Abby said. "Your mom will never have to know."

"Thanks," yelled Stacy. "Sorry about the money."

"It's my own fault," Abby said. She went into the bathroom.

"No it isn't," Stacy said. She rubbed more soap on the puppy's head. "We were in it together."

"I've been thinking," Abby said. "It doesn't matter if you're adopted. Look how much your parents love you."

"I know that," said Stacy. "It's not so much being adopted . . . if I am. I just wish my parents had told me." Stacy sighed. "Your brothers know all about their adoption."

"Shawn and Jimmy were older when it happened," Abby said. She heard the garage door open. "Sounds like your mom's home," she said. "I better leave."

"No, wait," said Stacy. "I've got an idea."

"What?" Abby pulled a towel off the rack and handed it to Stacy.

"I'm going to ask my mom some questions. And I want you to listen." Stacy drained the dirty bath water.

There were footsteps in the hallway. "Stacy, I'm home," said her mother.

"Coming!" called Stacy. She lifted Sunday Funnies out of the tub.

Abby helped dry him.

"Follow me," Stacy said.

Abby followed her friend to the kitchen.

Stacy pulled a sheet of paper out of a drawer. She sat down at the table. Abby did, too.

Stacy took a deep breath. "I need to talk to you, Mom."

"Sure, honey. What's up?"

Stacy shot a nervous look at Abby. "What happened on the day I was born?"

"What do you mean, dear?" her mother asked.

"I need to know for my homework," Stacy said. "Were you there?"

Stacy's mother looked at her. She set the dishes on the counter. "Of course I was."

"How soon did you see me?" Stacy asked.

"A few hours after you were born."

Stacy laughed. "A few hours? That's a long time to wait, don't you think?"

Her mother opened a drawer and took out a spoon. "Why do you ask?"

Abby looked at Stacy. She held her breath.

Stacy stood up. "What happened to my birth certificate?"

"I really don't know," her mother said. "But we need to set the table now."

"Did you take any pictures of me when I was born?" Stacy asked.

Mrs. Henry pushed her hair back. She sighed. "I think your father did."

Stacy wrote something on her paper. "Does he still have them?"

"It's late now, Stacy. You know how sloppy I am at keeping records sometimes. Can we please talk about this later?" her mother said.

Abby stood up. "I better go home now. See you tomorrow, Stacy."

Stacy scrunched up her face. "OK, Abby."

Abby felt funny. Stacy's eyes didn't look like things were OK.

They spelled trouble. Big trouble!

Abby felt like a jitterbug.

Something was crazy wrong!

Eight

After supper, Abby checked under her bed.

Good! The atlas was still there. Her sketch of South Korea marked the page. She stared at the map.

Then she looked at the teddy bear calendar on the wall. Only ten more days till Shawn's birthday!

Abby knelt beside her bed and prayed, "Please, Lord, help me get some money for my brother's birthday party."

■■■

The next day, Abby met Stacy in the lunch-room. They sat at a long table next to the wall.

Abby leaned against the wall. "I have an idea, Stacy. Why don't you call your dad?"

"I've been thinking about it," Stacy said. She dipped a spoon into her chocolate pudding.

The girls next to them traded sticks of gum.

"You could ask your dad to send some of your baby pictures," Abby suggested.

"Great idea," Stacy said.

"Maybe he knows something about your birth certificate," Abby said, smiling. She hoped her idea would help.

"You're a good friend, Abby Hunter," Stacy said.

Abby felt warm inside.

"I'm going to call a meeting of the Cul-de-Sac Kids," Stacy said.

"When? Why?"

"Tomorrow," said Stacy. "And don't ask so many questions." She had a sneaky smile.

"What's up?" Abby asked. She could see in her friend's face that something was!

"Wait and see," Stacy said. She went to dump her trash.

■■■

On Friday, everyone showed up at Dunkum's house. His real name was Edward Mifflin. He was a third-grade hotshot on the basketball court.

Dunkum had the biggest basement in the cul-de-sac. That's where the kids liked to meet—in their socks. All the sneakers were lined up beside the stairs.

Abby sat in a beanbag chair near the TV.

She was president. But today, Stacy was in charge.

The kids sat on the floor.

Stacy told them what her puppy had done. "Abby didn't want me to get in trouble. So she used up all of her money to replace the roast and the ice cream. Now she needs a loan from us. For something very important."

Carly wiggled. Her eyes danced. Abby could

tell she was having a hard time keeping the birthday secret.

Dunkum stood up. "Let's hear it for Abby. I'll loan her three bucks. Who will match it?"

Jason Birchall swayed back and forth. He could never sit still. Even with his medicine. "I don't have three, but how's two-fifty?" he asked.

"We'll take it," said Dunkum. He smiled at Dee Dee Winters. "What about you? Got any cash to loan?"

"Just fifty cents." She pulled out two quarters. "The tooth fairy came last night." She showed the hole where her tooth had been.

Carly scooted over beside her.

Shawn raised his hand. "I save money. I give money to Abby." He stood up and emptied his pockets.

Shawn handed the money to Dunkum.

Abby didn't want her brother's money. It was going for *his* cake! "Uh, that's plenty without Shawn's," she said quickly.

Eric Hagel whistled. "Hey, what about me? I have a dollar," he said. "And Abby doesn't ever have to pay me back."

"Thanks," Dunkum said, reaching for it.

Abby wished they would stop. God had answered her prayer with more than enough money for Shawn's cake. She waved her hands. "Yo, kids!"

"The president of the Cul-de-Sac Kids wants to speak," Stacy announced.

The kids got quiet. Even Carly and Dee Dee.

"Thanks for helping me out," Abby said. "I'll pay each of you back as soon as I can. Now, I want to invite everyone to a birthday party for my brother next Saturday. Come over after lunch."

Shawn's eyebrows shot up. Then he grinned.

The kids cheered. "All right, Shawn! Hurray for Abby!"

The meeting was over. The scramble for sneakers began.

Dee Dee got Carly's by mistake. They were red, too, but bigger.

After the kids left, Stacy sat beside Abby. "I'm going to call my father tonight," Stacy said.

Abby stretched her legs. "That's double dabble good!"

Stacy smiled. "I think it's time to ask him a few questions."

The girls got up and found their sneakers. Abby's were mismatched. One red, one blue.

"Be sure and tell me what he says," Abby said. She put the money in her jeans pocket. "Thanks for helping. You're a good friend, Stacy Henry."

Abby ran all the way home. She had a birthday party to plan. Things were definitely terrific.

Nothing could go wrong now!

Nine

The next morning, Abby dashed over to Stacy's. "Did you call your dad?"

Stacy stood in the doorway. She zipped up her jacket. "I chickened out."

"Oh," said Abby. She wished Stacy wasn't so nervous about it.

They rode their bikes to the store. It was time to buy the birthday stuff.

Abby couldn't make up her mind. Should she buy blue balloons? Or red ones?

"This is my Korean brother's first birthday in the United States," said Abby.

"Get him American colors," Stacy suggested.

So Abby bought red, white, and blue balloons.

Later, they hid the party stuff under Abby's bed. Then Stacy went home.

■ ■ ■

After lunch, Stacy phoned. "Can I come over?" She sounded excited.

"Sure," Abby said, pulling off her sneakers.

The doorbell rang. *Ding-dong!*

Abby ran to the front door in her socks.

Stacy flew inside and grabbed Abby's arm. "I'm *not* adopted!"

"How do you know?"

"I called my dad. He has my birth certificate. And he's going to send me a copy!"

They dashed upstairs to Abby's bedroom.

"And that's not all," Stacy said. "He wants to come visit me sometime."

Abby closed the door. This was super double dabble good!

Stacy sat on the rug. So did Abby.

"This is the best day of my life," Stacy said. She pulled off her sneakers. "The mystery of my birth is solved."

Abby laughed. "And *you* solved it!" She reached under the bed and pulled out a bag of balloons.

"If you need any help with the party, let me know," Stacy said. "I'm not the best detective, but I'm a good fixer-upper."

Abby ripped open the balloon bag. "Can you blow up balloons?"

"Sure," said Stacy. And she blew up a blue one. It made her face bright red.

Abby clapped for her. "I can't wait for the party."

Just then, Carly came into the room. She had pink bumps on her arms and face. She was moaning.

"Look who's got chicken pox," Stacy said.

"Oh no," Abby gasped. "Stay away from Shawn."

"That's right!" Stacy snapped. "If he gets them, there goes the party!"

Abby jumped up and led Carly off to her own room.

Ten

It was three days before Shawn's party. Little Jimmy was sick in bed with chicken pox. Itchy spots were in his nose and in his hair. They were nearly everywhere!

Dee Dee Winters had them, too. And Jason Birchall missed school.

Abby was worried. *Who's next?*

Two days before the party, Eric and Dunkum broke out with chicken pox. After supper, Shawn did, too.

"Rats!" Abby said to her mother. "Now we can't have the party."

"But you can still bake a cake," her mother said. "Shawn would like that."

The next day, Abby hurried to the kitchen.

She got out mixing bowls, eggs, and flour. Then baking powder, sugar, chocolate squares, and canned frosting.

She posted the pattern of South Korea on the refrigerator with a clown magnet. Next, she tiptoed to the boys' room. They were sound asleep. Good!

Back in the kitchen, she followed her mother's recipe. When she measured the flour and the sugar, some of it flew onto the floor. When she mixed the batter, it spilled, too. What a mess!

At last, she slid the cake pans into the oven and waited.

When the timer rang, Abby used the hot pads. The oven was very hot, and so were the cake pans. She placed them on the counter to cool.

Then Abby heard footsteps. She turned around. There was Jimmy, making flour footprints on the floor. Snow White was behind him, licking up spilled sugar.

Abby stared at her little brother. "What are you doing up?"

"Thirsty," Jimmy moaned.

Abby poured a glass of water. "Here," she

said, holding the glass out to him. "Now go back to bed."

"Not tired," he said, scratching his spots.

"Don't scratch," Abby said. "It'll make marks."

He walked to the refrigerator, tracking flour everywhere. Reaching for the map of South Korea, Jimmy slipped and fell.

"Ouch!" he cried.

Abby helped him back to bed. Shawn was still asleep.

Whew! Close call.

Gotta hurry, thought Abby, tiptoeing back to the kitchen.

She turned the first cake pan upside down. It was so hot it burned her fingers. The cake came out in a crumbly mess on the plate.

Oh no! What's wrong? she thought.

Then she remembered Stacy—the fixer-upper. Abby called her best friend on the phone. She came right over.

"I want it to look like South Korea," Abby said, pointing to the map in her hand. "Shawn's birthday is tomorrow!"

Stacy looked at the drawing. "So *this* is the secret you were keeping from me."

"Please help me, Stacy," Abby whispered. "I'll never keep secrets from you again, I promise."

Stacy smiled. "It's a deal. Now, first of all, the pans have to cool before you dump out the cake," she explained. "But I think I can fix your mess."

Abby watched as Stacy worked.

Bit by bit, she pieced the cake together with canned frosting. But the cake had ugly bumps and ridges in it.

It looked more like the Grand Canyon than South Korea!

Later, the second cake pan was cool enough. Stacy turned it over, but the cake was stuck!

Stacy groaned. "Why didn't you butter and flour the pan first?"

"I thought I did."

Stacy tried one more time to get the cake out of the pan. But it fell out in pieces.

Abby looked at the cake in horror. "Oh no!" she cried.

"Oh, forget it. Just get me a streamer," Stacy said.

"What for?"

"To hold the cake together," Stacy said.

Abby had never heard of such a thing. Did Stacy really know what she was doing?

Abby ran to her room to get the red streamers. There was no time to waste.

Eleven

Abby rushed back to the kitchen with red streamers and tape.

Stacy wrapped the streamer around the pieces of cake. She stuck tape on the end. Then she stepped back to have a look.

Abby didn't know what to think of the repair job. "Shouldn't we frost it all over?" Abby asked.

"When it cools some more." Stacy slid the cake into the freezer. When she closed the door, she leaned against it. "Remember that pot roast you bought with your own money?"

Abby felt jittery. "Sure, why?"

"Well, my mother noticed it was a different brand. So I told her what we did." Stacy paused. "I told her everything."

"I'm glad you did," Abby said. "I knew we were wrong."

Stacy grinned and washed her hands. "She wants you to come for supper tonight."

"She does?"

Stacy laughed. "We're having your pot roast."

Abby's jitters were gone. "I'll tell your mother I'm sorry in person," she said.

Then she set the timer. In fifteen minutes, she would check the cake.

When Stacy left, Abby sat at the kitchen table. She thought about Shawn's chicken pox. She thought about the birthday cake. What an icky mess it was—even with the red streamer holding it together. The white frosting could never hide the ugly mess. It still looked more like the Grand Canyon than South Korea.

Then Abby had an idea. She searched in the pantry and found what she needed. A bag of red cherry chips.

Abby's cake still had a chance. It would be

first-rate after all. Her cake could have the chicken pox!

The red cherry chips would hide the lumpy, bumpy cake. It was perfect!

Abby danced a jig around the kitchen.

The buzzer rang.

Abby jigged to the freezer and took out the cake.

Ready!

■ ■ ■

The next day was Shawn's birthday. Abby got up early and decorated the kitchen with red, white, and blue balloons. Even though the party was off, she wanted to surprise Shawn.

After lunch, the doorbell rang. When Abby opened the door, there stood the Cul-de-Sac Kids. Chicken pox and all!

"Surprise!" they shouted. "Surprise on you, Abby Hunter!"

Letting her friends inside, Abby giggled. It was definitely a good surprise.

The kids cheered when they saw the kitchen.

Abby gave everyone a red marker. "Let's

put red spots everywhere. We'll give everything the chicken pox!" she said.

And that's what they did.

The balloons and the napkins were spotted. Even the streamers had pox dots!

Abby put red sticker dots on the dog. Now Snow White had chicken pox, too. She barked and ran around in circles.

Abby's mother invited everyone to sit down. Then Shawn peeked around the corner in his pajamas. He grinned at his spotty friends.

"Surprise!" they shouted. "Happy birthday!"

Abby pulled out a chair for her brother. It was at the head of the table. Then she carried in the lumpy, bumpy cake with white frosting. And red cherry chip chicken pox spots.

Mother lit the birthday candles. They were white with red polka dots. "Happy, happy birthday, son," she said.

"Make a wish," Abby said.

Shawn closed his eyes. There were spots on his eyelids.

Then Shawn blew out nine candles on the first try.

Everyone cheered. Abby wanted to dance.

It was a super itchy-gitchy Saturday, so the party was short. But it didn't matter.

The Cul-de-Sac Kids said it was the best pox party ever!

BOOK 3

The Crazy Christmas Angel Mystery

To
Mary Erickson.
Your cheerful heart
and gentle words
make me smile.

One

It was five days before Christmas break. Eric Hagel shoved his feet into his snow boots. He peeked out his bedroom window. A full moon made the snow twinkle. He shivered thinking about his paper route.

Downstairs, Eric stuffed newspapers into his canvas bag. He wrapped his scarf around his neck and zipped up his fleece jacket. Pushing his earmuffs on, Eric stepped out into the cold morning.

Then he saw it—a moving van parked in front of the empty house next door. Snow was stuck to its huge tires.

Eric peeked around the porch. *What a giant moving van*, he thought. *There must be a bunch of kids moving in!*

Ducking behind the tree in his yard, Eric watched. A man with a long nose and a pointy chin shouted orders to the movers. He waved his cane in the cold air, like someone directing traffic.

Eric dashed through the snow. He slid behind a hedge close to the garage. Now he could see better.

He watched as the man's long coat billowed out like a cape.

"Put the boxes in the living room," the man said. His voice sounded gruff—and a little scary.

Eric glanced at his watch . . . 6:30. Plenty of time before school started.

The movers carried in a sofa and chair. And beds and lamps and boxes. Eric kept waiting for some kids to show up. Surely the new neighbor didn't live by himself. Surely he had a family . . . or someone.

A gust of wind blew Eric's green scarf across his eyes. He pushed it back quickly.

The old man paced back and forth. Then he stopped. He was staring at the hedge. Could he see Eric hiding behind it?

Quickly, Eric stuffed his scarf inside his

coat. He pushed his newspaper bag down. He could feel his heart thumping.

The old man shuffled to the edge of the sidewalk.

Eric shivered.

Then the old man mumbled something, but Eric couldn't understand it.

Maybe he was having a bad day. Moving was like that sometimes.

Eric remembered the day he moved to Blossom Hill Lane. It was no fun. Not till he met the Cul-de-Sac Kids. Now there was no better place on earth!

"We stick together, no matter what," Abby Hunter had always said. And it was true from the first time he met them. The Cul-de-Sac Kids were true friends.

Eric decided he would be the one to welcome the new kids. The ones he hoped were moving into the house at the end of Blossom Hill Lane. He would do it—even if he had to spy a little first.

Two

Eric watched the old man go inside. He wanted to ask where his family was. But it was time to deliver papers.

Eric got up and brushed the snow off his knees. He crossed the street to Stacy Henry's house. A light was on in the kitchen. Stacy's mother was probably getting her Crock-Pot ready. She worked long hours.

Eric opened the storm door. He tried not to shake the Christmas wreath. Then he put the newspaper inside.

Abby Hunter's house, next door, was dark except for Christmas lights. Around each window, red, white, and green lights flashed on and off.

Next came Dunkum's house. His real name was Edward Mifflin, but nobody called him that. He was Dunkum, the hottest third-grade basketball player around.

Eric opened the storm door. He placed the newspaper inside.

Eric did the same thing at each house. He wanted to keep the papers dry for the customers.

Someone was up early at Dee Dee Winters' house. Probably her dad. Mr. Winters had a long drive to work in the mountains.

Eric turned left at the end of the cul-de-sac. He had a bunch more houses to go.

The sky was turning grayish pink. It would be dawn soon.

■■■

At last, Eric headed home. His mother's hot blueberry oatmeal was waiting.

In the corner of the kitchen, his grandpa's birds chirped their morning song. Three canaries and a pair of parakeets.

Soon, Eric heard Abby Hunter's whistle. The Cul-de-Sac Kids were heading for Blossom Hill School.

Eric's mother hugged him. Then he pulled on his boots, jacket, and scarf. Again.

He dashed out the front door, letting it slam.

Across the street, Abby and her new Korean brothers, Shawn and Jimmy, packed clumps of snow into balls.

Stacy Henry hid behind her snowman. She laughed as the snowballs flew at her.

Dee Dee Winters was halfway down the cul-de-sac, skipping through piles of snow. She strapped on her red backpack. It was probably filled with Christmas cookies for her teacher. Dee Dee was the best first-grade cookie baker ever.

Carly Hunter, Abby's little sister, followed Dee Dee. They were best friends. They giggled and kicked the snow in the street.

Dunkum and Jason Birchall raced and slid. They zoomed up and down Dunkum's driveway. After school they would go sledding down mean and steep Blossom Hill, three blocks away. Eric would go, too.

Eric hurried to catch up. His pants still stuck to his knees from kneeling in the snow, spying on the new neighbor. "Wait!" he called to Dunkum and Jason.

Abby ran up to him. "What took you so long?"

Eric pointed to the house with the moving van. "I wanted to see who was moving in."

Stacy tossed a snowball to Abby. Abby caught it and threw it back.

"Were you spying, Eric?" Stacy asked, grinning.

"Just welcoming the new neighbors," Eric said, grinning back.

"There's only one," said Stacy.

Eric pulled at his wet jeans. "Who says?"

"Abby does," Stacy insisted.

"You sure there are no kids?" Eric asked.

Stacy nodded. "For now, Shawn and Jimmy are the newest kids on the block." She chased Abby's brothers. They were too fast for her.

Eric tramped through the deepest snow he could find. He grumbled under his breath. "I hope they're wrong," he whispered. "Who wants to live all alone?"

Eric felt sorry for the old man. He remembered when he and his mother were alone. It was after his father died in Germany. Then his mother invited Grandpa to live with them. That's when they came to the United States.

That was two years ago—when Eric was in first grade.

Eric turned around and looked down the cul-de-sac. Just as he did, the man with the pointy chin stood in the window of his house. He was leaning on his cane and seemed to be looking right at Eric.

Eric froze in place.

The man *was* looking at him!

Eric shivered. His stomach flip-flopped.

Then the curtains closed.

Eric turned around. He ran to catch up with his friends. But all he could think of was the man at the end of the cul-de-sac. *Why is he alone? Is he as creepy as he looks?*

The bell rang as Eric started across the schoolyard. "Wait for me!" he called.

"Hurry up," shouted Dunkum. "We'll be late!"

Eric slid down the sidewalk and dashed into the school.

Three

Eric pounded down the hall toward the third grade. He pushed the door open. Miss Hershey was writing on the board.

Eric pulled off his boots and hung up his jacket. Then he slid into his seat behind Dunkum. He tapped his friend on the shoulder.

Dunkum turned around. "What?"

"There's an old man at the end of the block. And he's, uh, real scary," Eric whispered.

Dunkum frowned. "There is?"

Eric described the old man's long dark coat, the cane, his face and—

"Eric Hagel," Miss Hershey said.

Eric looked up. "I'm here."

Miss Hershey was calling roll. Eric would

have to tell Dunkum the rest of the story at recess.

Abby was passing back the spelling tests from last week. Eric made a 100. Yes!

He leaned up to look at Dunkum's. But Dunkum put his hand over the grade at the top of his paper.

Too late. Eric had seen it.

"Don't worry," Eric said. "I'll help you drill for the next test."

Dunkum picked at the eraser on his pencil. "OK," he muttered.

Eric looked at the new spelling list. The words were *yule, candlelight, carols, wreath, decoration, tinsel, holly, angels, mystery*, and *candy cane.*

Mystery? Eric stared at the word. What was it doing on the Christmas spelling list?

Squeezing his pencil, Eric began to write the words in his best printing.

It wasn't easy. Eric kept seeing the old man's face. It showed up when he wrote the words on the list. It appeared when he wrote his name on the right side.

Eric rubbed his eyes. He had to get the man's face out of his mind!

He looked at the flag. He counted to ten under his breath. Then he looked at Miss Hershey. Her bright red-and-green Christmas sweater might help him forget the scary face.

"Eric, are you all right?" Miss Hershey asked.

He nodded. Everything would be all right soon, he told himself.

■■■

After school, Eric went sledding down Blossom Hill with Dunkum and Jason. Eric forgot about the scary face. It was almost dark when the boys headed home.

"Are you still gonna help me with my spelling?" Dunkum asked Eric.

"Sure am," Eric said. "But I have to get home after that to finish my book report."

"What's your book about?" Jason asked.

"It's a mystery," Eric answered.

"Sounds good," Jason said. "I like mysteries."

Dunkum's sled got stuck in the snow. He pulled hard on the rope. "Mysteries are OK, I guess."

Jason laughed. "The scarier, the better."

"Don't they give you bad dreams?" asked Dunkum.

"Sometimes," Jason said. "But if I pray before I go to bed, it's better."

Eric pulled his scarf tighter. "Why don't you just skip the scary stuff?"

Dunkum said, "Yeah, remember that Bible verse about only thinkin' on good stuff?"

"The Bible says that?" Eric said.

Dunkum smiled. "I learned it when I first went to Abby's church. You should come see the Christmas program. I'm gonna be Joseph this year."

"Who's Mary?" Jason asked.

"Abby Hunter," Dunkum said. His cheeks turned red. But not just from the cold.

Eric scooped up some snow and licked it.

Four

Eric pulled his sled toward his house. Before going inside, he glanced next door.

The moving van was gone, and the garage door was closed. Everything looked dark . . . till someone lit a candle in the living room. And another and another. Soon, the room was filled with a spooky glow.

What was going on? Didn't the old man have electricity?

I saw lights this morning, Eric thought.

Leaving his sled on the porch, Eric kicked his boots off inside the front door. He smelled German sausage. Yum!

Eric's mother was setting the dining room table. Grandpa was talking to his birds.

Eric went to the kitchen to wash his hands. They were frosty from sledding.

His mother came into the kitchen. "I've been thinking about inviting Mr. Tressler for supper sometime."

Grandpa turned away from the birdcages. "Who?"

"Our new neighbor," Mrs. Hagel said.

"Very thoughtful," said Grandpa. "I'd like to meet the old fellow."

Eric dried his hands and hurried into the dining room. He didn't know what to say. How could he tell his mother he was scared of Mr. Tressler?

Eric's mother brought in the steaming sausage, and potato salad mixed with caraway seeds.

Eric's grandfather chuckled. "I think those birds want a taste of sausage."

Eric pulled his chair out and sat down. Grandpa was bird-crazy.

"Give them some caraway seeds instead," Eric suggested.

■ ■ ■

Before dessert, Eric's mother brought out a handful of candles. She lit all of them. The dining room glowed with a magical golden light.

Eric stared at the candles. There were twelve. They reminded him of the light in Mr. Tressler's spooky living room.

"Only twelve days till Christmas," Eric's mother said. "I hope to finish my shopping this weekend."

Eric glanced at the candle in front of his plate. He hadn't even started shopping. Oh well, there was plenty of time left.

He daydreamed into the candlelight. Suddenly, the old man's face popped out! It was the same scary face he'd seen that morning.

Yikes! Eric rubbed his eyes.

"Are you tired?" his mother asked.

"No," Eric said quickly. He didn't want to be sent off to bed early. That would spoil his plans to spy on the mystery man.

Five

After supper, Eric hurried to Dunkum's house. The Christmas spelling list was ready.

Eric gave the first word. "Spell *Yule*."

Dunkum tried and missed. He left the "e" off the end. "I don't get it," he said.

Eric held up a dictionary. "Find it in here."

Dunkum looked and looked. At last, he said, "Here it is. It means *you will*. *You will* shouldn't be on a Christmas spelling list."

"Not y-o-u-'-l-l," Eric said. "Y-u-l-e is a Christmas word. Here, let me show you." He found the word in the dictionary. Eric let Dunkum read the meaning.

"Yule means Christmas?" asked Dunkum.

Eric nodded. "In Germany, where I was

born, people used to burn Yule logs at Christmas. It's a giant piece of firewood. Sometimes the whole trunk of a tree."

"Wow! The whole trunk?" said Dunkum.

"Yep."

"How does it fit into the fireplace?" asked Dunkum.

"Our fireplaces can't hold a Yule log, but in the old days they could. Now my mom lights candles instead."

Eric looked at the next word on the list. *Candlelight*. "I'll give you a hint," he said. "This word is two words put together. It's a compound word."

First try, Dunkum spelled it right.

Eric drilled his friend on all the words. When they came to *mystery*, Eric scratched his head. "I wonder why Miss Hershey put this word on the list."

"Maybe she knows about the first Christmas," Dunkum replied.

"What do you mean?" Eric asked.

"Well, the first Christmas was a true mystery. Only God could have set it up."

Eric closed the dictionary. "Huh?"

"For one thing, Joseph and Mary didn't

live in Bethlehem. But God knew way ahead of time that Jesus was gonna be born there." Dunkum sat down beside Eric on the floor.

"What else?" Eric said.

"Jesus was God's son—but he was also a man. That's a good mystery for you," said Dunkum.

"Yeah," said Eric. "You're right."

"That's not all," said Dunkum. "The first Christmas was about presents—the best one of all. A baby boy named Jesus."

"Sounds like you really have this stuff down," Eric said.

"I learned it at church," Dunkum said.

Eric thought about the spelling list. "Does Miss Hershey go, too?" he asked.

Dunkum stood up. "I've never seen her there. But I have a feeling she goes to church somewhere."

It was time to leave. Eric had important plans. He headed straight for Mr. Tressler's house. The moon was as big as a basketball. Full moons were like that.

Just then, Dee Dee's kitten jumped out of the bushes. Eric stopped. A house cat could freeze to death outside. Eric ran after him. "Come here, Mister Whiskers."

Meow. The cat headed down the sidewalk to Mr. Tressler's. Leaping over mounds of snow, Mister Whiskers seemed to know where he was going. Straight to the old man's front porch!

Eric's heart was pounding hard. "Here, kitty, kitty," he called softly. Eric tiptoed through the snow, reaching out for the fluffy gray cat.

Then Mister Whiskers leaped onto the windowsill. Boldly, he pranced across.

This is horrible! thought Eric. Then he looked up.

He could see the old man's shadow in the window. By the light of a dozen candles, Mr. Tressler was putting up a Christmas tree.

Eric couldn't see clearly through the sheer curtain. But he could see Mr. Tressler's long nose and pointy chin.

Eric shivered in the darkness. The whole thing was creepy. He moved closer to get a better look.

Candles flickered in the window. Moon shadows danced on the snow. Then Mister

Whiskers meowed like a trumpet in the stillness.

"Be quiet!" Eric shouted.

The porch light flashed.

Eric spun around and ran for his life!

Six

Eric slammed his front door. He leaned hard against it, gasping for breath. He was safe!

"What's the matter?" his mother asked.

Eric tossed his jacket onto the hook in the closet. His chest moved up and down. He could hardly talk.

"Eric, are you all right?" she said.

He waved his hands in front of his face. "It's Mister Whiskers . . . he's out there . . . in the cold . . . somewhere."

"That poor little thing?"

Eric nodded. "I was trying to catch him and take him home." It was only half the truth.

"Well, I think you'd better bundle up and

try again." She pulled his coat down off the hook and held it up.

Eric didn't say a word. He was too scared. Too scared to go back out there and look for Mister Whiskers. Closing the door behind him, Eric stayed on his front porch. It felt safer there.

He looked at Mr. Tressler's house. The porch light was still on. But Mister Whiskers was nowhere to be seen.

Slowly, Eric crept into the night.

He studied the shadows behind the living room curtains. It looked like Mr. Tressler was decorating his tree.

If only he had Grandpa's field glasses. His grandpa used them for bird-watching in the spring. Eric wished he had them now. He could stay far enough away from the old man's house.

Eric went back inside. He asked Grandpa for the field glasses—very politely.

"Why do you want them?" Grandpa asked.

"They might help me find Mister Whiskers." Eric felt bad about lying to Grandpa.

"How can you find a cat in the dark?" his grandfather asked.

"Please, just let me try?" Eric pleaded.

Grandpa pulled himself up out of his chair. He muttered something and went upstairs.

Eric crossed his fingers, hoping.

When his grandpa came down, Eric saw the field glasses. Yes!

Promising to take care of them, Eric dashed outside. Now for a good hiding place.

He looked around the cul-de-sac. His eyes stopped in front of Stacy's house. There stood her fat snowman. It was perfect!

He crossed the street and headed for the snowman.

Crouching down, Eric held the glasses. He turned the dial. Slowly, Mr. Tressler's living room came into view. Candles flickered everywhere.

Through the curtains, Eric saw Mr. Tressler hang a string of Christmas lights. He wondered if the old man was smiling. He wished he could see his face. Then Eric remembered the scary face and changed his mind.

Mr. Tressler hung up some round ornaments. Last, the Christmas angel.

Eric could almost hear Mr. Tressler grunting and groaning as he reached up, just like

Grandpa. The angel came to rest at the top. The old man stepped back for a long look.

Then the most shocking thing happened. Mr. Tressler stepped closer to the tree. He reached up to touch the angel and . . .

It began to fly! Around and around the room, it glided.

Eric felt glued to the spot behind the snowman. Reading about stuff like this was one thing. But seeing it? Wait till he told the other Cul-de-Sac Kids!

He stood on his toes for a better look. The angel was still doing its thing. Drifting through the air, around the living room!

"Whatcha doin'?" someone said behind him.

Eric jumped a foot high.

It was Dee Dee Winters.

"You should *never* sneak up behind someone like that!" Eric scolded.

"Mister Whiskers is lost!"

"I know. I'll help you in a second," Eric said. "Here, look through these first." He held up the field glasses for Dee Dee. "See that angel flying around?"

Dee Dee was silent as she watched. Little

puffs of air came out of her nose. Finally, she said, "Wow! What's happenin' over there?"

"Crazy, isn't it?" Eric said.

Dee Dee nodded. Her eyes grew bigger and bigger. "I've never seen a real angel before."

"Me neither."

Dee Dee was shivering hard.

"Come on, I'll help you find your cat," Eric said.

They crossed the street together.

Meow. Meow.

Eric stopped. "Did you hear that?"

Dee Dee called, "Here, Mister Whiskers."

More meows. Shaky, shivery meows.

They found frosty Mister Whiskers under Eric's porch. Dee Dee bent down and picked him up. "Thank you, Eric."

"It was nothing," he said. "Hurry home. And be careful who you talk to about Mr. Tressler's angel."

"I'm gonna call Carly right away." And she turned around and left.

Eric darted into his house. He had to make some phone calls, too.

The crazy Christmas angel was stranger than any mystery he had ever read!

160

Seven

Eric called Dunkum first. "You'll never believe what I saw tonight," he bragged.

Dunkum was all ears. He wanted to see for himself. Abby and Jason and Stacy did, too.

So . . . Eric had a plan. The Cul-de-Sac Kids would have a meeting tomorrow night—behind the snowman in Stacy's yard.

Terrific!

He zipped off to his room to do his homework. The book report was due tomorrow. He would have to write fast to get it done.

Knock, knock.

"Come in," Eric called.

It was Grandpa. He wanted his field glasses back.

Gulp! Eric scratched his head. He must

161

have left them outside. His face was getting hot. It was his own fault. His, and that crazy angel's!

"Wait, Grandpa. I'll be right back," Eric said. He flew down the stairs, yanked at his coat, and ran outside.

Eric scrambled across the street to the snowman. He leaned over to look. Nothing.

He got down on his hands and knees. He patted the snowy ground. Nothing.

Grandpa's field glasses were gone!

Eric felt the lump in his throat grow bigger. He stood up and leaned against the snowman. He brushed the snow off his jeans.

When he looked up, the field glasses were staring at him. Carefully, he picked them off the snowman's shoulder.

Eric held them up and looked through them.

Whew! They were okay.

While he was checking them, something caught his eye. Across the street at Mr. Tressler's house, things were crazy. Crazier than ever!

Eric adjusted the field glasses. Could it be true? Were his eyes playing tricks?

BEVERLY LEWIS

Slowly, Eric moved toward Mr. Tressler's house. He got as close as the hedge.

Field glasses do not lie.

The angels had multiplied! Dozens were flying around the old man. He was swaying this way and that way. Mr. Tressler was dancing with the angels. It looked like he was having the time of his life.

Eric wanted to watch forever. Something deep inside him sprang up. It was a strange, warm feeling that wouldn't go away. He knew he had to meet Mr. Tressler. Face-to-face!

Eric rushed to the old man's front porch. He shook as he stuffed the field glasses into his pocket. More than anything, he wanted to ring the doorbell. But his finger wouldn't move. He forced his arm up—shaking with fear.

"Eric!" It was Grandpa's voice.

Eric jumped a foot. The second time tonight. He leaped over the snowy walkway to his house. He held up the field glasses. "Here they are, Grandpa."

Grandpa frowned.

"I'm sorry about your glasses," Eric said. He was sorry about something else, too. Not getting to meet Mr. Tressler.

"Those glasses were expensive," Grandpa said, shaking his finger at Eric.

Eric looked up at Grandpa's soft blue eyes. "It won't happen again. I promise."

"And that's the truth," Grandpa muttered. He climbed the stairs, grunting all the way.

So much for borrowing Grandpa's stuff. Eric dashed upstairs to finish his book report.

Then he thought of something. If he hadn't left Grandpa's glasses outside, he might have missed the strange sight next door. The angels had multiplied!

Now Eric had a big mystery on his hands. And he didn't know what to do about it.

Then he had an idea. It might not solve the mystery, but it would show a little kindness.

Eight

The next morning, Eric trudged through the snow. He headed to Mr. Tressler's house to deliver a newspaper free of charge. Eric would pay for it himself, out of his earnings.

Eric tiptoed up the porch steps. He turned the handle on the storm door. And he placed the paper in the space between the two doors.

Inside, a cuckoo clock sang out the time. Six cuckoos in a row.

Eric checked his watch. Six o'clock, right on the dot. He turned to leave, but the sound of a flute stopped him. It was coming from inside Mr. Tressler's house.

Eric froze in his tracks.

Mr. Tressler plays the flute.

Eric listened.

It was music for the angels! He chuckled to himself as the silvery sounds floated around him.

He leaned against the porch railing and felt lucky—the only one to hear the magic. He breathed it in and held it close.

Then the music stopped. And the front door opened. Eric sprang off the porch and dashed down the street.

■ ■ ■

After supper, the Cul-de-Sac Kids met in Stacy's front yard as planned. Abby was president, so she called the meeting to order. That was easy. The only reason for the meeting was to see the angels at Mr. Tressler's house.

Dunkum set up his telescope. Eric had first look. The angels were flying, all right. And Mr. Tressler was prancing and swaying.

Carly and Dee Dee took turns looking through the telescope. Shawn and Jimmy were next.

Jason couldn't wait his turn. "If there's a man dancing with angels, I've got to see it!"

He walked across the street for a closer look. Dunkum followed.

Eric stayed behind with Abby and Stacy, near the snowman.

"I should invite Mr. Tressler to our Christmas play," Abby said. "He could appear to the shepherds and bring his heavenly host."

Stacy laughed. "Good idea."

"What do you think makes them fly, Eric?" Abby asked after her turn.

"Batteries, probably," said Eric. But he didn't know. Not really. He watched as the angels circled Mr. Tressler's head.

Carly asked, "Do the batteries ever run down?"

"Sooner or later," Eric said, like he knew.

Just then, Dunkum and Jason came running. "Huddle up," Dunkum called.

The kids grabbed one another's arms and made a circle.

Dunkum had a plan. "Let's take a Christmas present to Mr. Tressler. Then we can find out what's going on in there."

"We've done enough spying," said Abby. "Let's sing Christmas carols for him. To welcome him to the cul-de-sac."

Everyone liked that idea. Everyone but Eric.

"I sing flat," Eric said.

"You could whistle," Abby suggested.

Leave it to Abby, thought Eric.

"Someone needs to introduce us after we sing," Abby said.

The kids looked at Eric.

"Why me?" Eric said.

"You got us out here," said Dunkum.

"Yeah, hurry up, it's cold," said Dee Dee.

Eric didn't want to do the talking. He didn't want to whistle Christmas carols. Besides, what if Mr. Tressler was real creepy and scared everyone away?

What then?

Nine

It's too late to go caroling now," Eric said. He was chickening out.

Abby stuck up for him. "Eric's right—besides, we need to practice first."

"How about everyone giving Mr. Tressler a gift? I'll make him a Christmas card," Stacy said. She was good at that.

"Definitely," said Abby.

"Don't forget the Christmas cookies," Dee Dee piped up.

Shawn wanted to give something, too. "I teach Mr. Tressler Korean folk tune."

Jimmy jumped up and down. "I sing, too!"

"Hey, great idea," said Dunkum.

"What about you?" Eric asked him. "What will you bring?"

Dunkum laughed. "Maybe I could write a poem about angels and mysteries. You know, from the Christmas spelling list."

Eric liked that. So did the others.

Jason couldn't stand still. He was like that when his ADD medicine wore off. "I could dance with Mr. Tressler's angels," said Jason. He jigged around the snowman.

Dee Dee giggled. "Me too!"

"If we sing the carols loudly enough, he might open the door," said Jason. "Then we can see those flying Christmas angels of his."

"Wait a minute," Carly spoke up. "I thought we were doing it to be friendly—*not* to spy."

Abby put her arm around her little sister. Carly grinned up at Abby in the moonlight.

The moonlight reminded Eric of Mr. Tressler's flute. That strange, warm feeling stirred inside him again. Maybe caroling for Mr. Tressler wasn't such a bad idea. Maybe he would give the old man a gift after all.

"I want to give our new neighbor something he'll never forget," Eric said.

"What is it?" the kids shouted.

"A friend," Eric said. He was thinking of his grandpa.

"Now everyone has something to give," said Abby. "Meet tomorrow after school at Dunkum's."

The kids scattered and went home.

Eric still wasn't sure about those angels. Did they run on batteries? Maybe not. Maybe Mr. Tressler was a true angel keeper. If so, Grandpa might be just the friend for him.

Sometimes, late at night, Eric could hear Grandpa talking to God. Some people called it praying. But with Grandpa, it was just plain talking.

Eric went to his room and put on his pajamas. He thought about Mr. Tressler. How could the old man dance with angels and still be so creepy?

Ten

It was December 15th.

After school, the Cul-de-Sac Kids met at Dunkum's. They practiced five songs five times in a row. "Silent Night" and "Jingle Bells" were good, but "Angels We Have Heard on High" was the best.

Eric whistled. Jason jigged. And Abby said they sounded double dabble good.

■■■

The next night, the kids lined up on Mr. Tressler's porch. Candles burned in the window. No one moved. Eric took a deep breath and pressed the doorbell.

When the porch light came on, the kids

started to sing "Joy to the World." Eric whistled along.

Slowly, the door opened.

There stood the old man without a smile. He reached for his cane!

Eric froze.

Mr. Tressler raised his cane in the air.

He's gonna chase us away! thought Eric.

Instead, the cane began to wave in time to the music. Mr. Tressler kept it up through "Silent Night" and "Frosty the Snowman."

But then, Mr. Tressler left.

What should they do?

Eric started whistling "Jingle Bells" as loudly as he could.

The old man came back with his flute. He began to play along, his eyes closed.

Eric felt a lump in his throat. The old man wasn't scary. Not one bit!

At the end, the kids clapped.

Mr. Tressler bowed low. "Thank you kindly," he said. "And you—what voices! You sound like the angels."

Angels! Eric peeked around the corner. He didn't see any angels. Had the batteries run down?

Abby pointed to Eric. It was time for him to talk. He introduced Stacy Henry first.

Stacy gave Mr. Tressler a glittery gold angel Christmas card. It was made from white construction paper.

"Welcome to our cul-de-sac," she said.

"Thank you, dear," said Mr. Tressler.

Eric pointed to Dee Dee Winters and said her name.

She handed him a basket of Christmas cookies. "I hope you like angel cookies."

Carly stood beside her. "She made them, and I sprinkled them." The girls giggled.

The old man nodded. "Thank you, indeed."

Eric said, "Now Shawn and Jimmy Hunter want to teach you a Korean folk song."

The boys started to sing. The rest of the kids tried to join in on the chorus. Everyone clapped at the end. Even Mr. Tressler.

Dunkum seemed shy when his turn came. "I made up a poem for you."

Eric could see the words *angel* and *mystery* on the paper. They were spelled right. Good for Dunkum!

Abby Hunter smiled when Eric introduced her. "I have a gift for you, but you must come

to my church on Christmas Eve to get it. It's the Christmas play. I'm going to be Mary."

Mr. Tressler smiled for the first time. "Why, thank you, I'd be delighted."

Jason Birchall was next. He couldn't stand still. "Want a fast dance or a slow one?" he asked.

"As you wish," Mr. Tressler said.

Jason began his jig. It looked like he was making it up as he went.

Then Mr. Tressler began to play his flute. It was "Jingle Bells" with lots of extra notes.

Jason's jig got better and better.

At the end, Mr. Tressler said, "Now I have a surprise for all of you."

Eric peeked through the storm door. He could see Mr. Tressler heading for the kitchen. But he didn't see any angels.

What was going on?

Eleven

Eric heard a soft cooing sound.

Mr. Tressler was coming through the living room. Eric leaned forward to see.

What was that on his shoulders?

Eric couldn't help it. He stared.

Mr. Tressler stood in the doorway. He was covered with white doves! They perched on his shoulders. And on his head. When he cupped his hands, three flew into them.

So these are the angels! thought Eric.

The birds seemed so comfortable around the old man. It was like he was their trusted friend.

Dee Dee's eyes grew wide.

Carly giggled.

Abby's jaw dropped two feet.

Stacy whispered, "Wow!"

Dunkum scratched his head and stared.

Shawn and Jimmy watched silently.

Jason blinked his eyes faster than ever.

Softly, Mr. Tressler began to whistle. The doves cooed along. Eric could see their short legs under their round bodies. What a strange sight.

Doves do look like tiny angels, thought Eric. *All in white, with big wings*.

Eric felt good inside. Mr. Tressler wasn't like anyone he'd ever met. Except maybe for Grandpa.

Grandpa loved birds—that was no secret. And sometimes, he did strange things, too. Like tramping around in the spring, spying on birds with his field glasses.

Mr. Tressler stopped whistling. "Merry Christmas, kids," he said, waving his arms. The doves flew to the Christmas tree. They perched on the branches.

The kids shouted, "Merry Christmas, Mr. Tressler!"

The new neighbor wore the widest grin on Blossom Hill Lane.

Eric whispered to him, "You whistle good."

The old man winked at him. "So do you."

"Want to come caroling . . . uh, whistling with us?" Eric asked.

Mr. Tressler reached for his cane. And his long brown coat. It looked just fine. Not creepy at all.

First stop, Eric's house.

Eric pressed the doorbell. He stood beside Mr. Tressler. They whistled while the others sang "Silent Night." They sounded good.

Grandpa came to the door. Eric introduced him to Mr. Tressler. Grandpa gave Eric a big hug. Then he grabbed his coat and hat. He joined the group as they caroled around the cul-de-sac.

Eric was so happy, he stopped whistling and tried to sing. It sounded flat, but it didn't matter. Mr. Tressler would never have to be alone again. The Cul-de-Sac Kids could be the old man's family!

Mr. Tressler's cane danced in the air as the carolers went from house to house.

Soon, they were back at the old man's home. He invited Eric's grandfather inside for coffee.

The Cul-de-Sac Kids waved good-bye to them. "Merry Christmas!" they shouted.

"And a merry Christmas to all of you," Mr. Tressler said, waving his cane. He was out of breath, but a smile burst across his long face.

Before the two men reached the porch, Eric was whistling again. It was time for his favorite carol—"Angels We Have Heard on High."

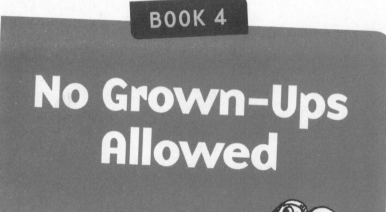

BOOK 4

No Grown-Ups
Allowed

This book is dedicated
in loving memory
to
my grandmother,
Zelma Elaine Jones
(1906–1994).
Her chocolate chip cookies
were the best
in the world,
because she mixed them
with love.

One

Jason Birchall stared at the valentine box on the kitchen table. He could almost taste the juicy chocolates. Cherry filled, caramel filled, coconut . . .

"Jason," his mother called. "Come here, please."

He backed away from the heart-shaped box. He didn't want his mother to know what he was thinking. Snitching thoughts!

"Coming," Jason answered.

His mother sat on the sofa in the living room. "Let's talk," she said.

But Jason's mind was on something else. He was thinking about ooey-gooey chocolates.

"We're going out of town for Valentine's

day," his mother began. "And Grandma Birchall will stay with you from Friday until Sunday."

Jason whined, "Oh, Mom. A whole weekend with Grandma?"

His mother frowned. "Now, Jason, you know better than that. Your grandma will take good care of you."

Jason quickly changed the subject. "Can I stay up late on Friday night?"

His mother shook her head. "You must get your rest, Jason. It's important."

"But, Mom!"

"Jason," she said firmly, "you will go to bed at your regular time. I don't want you to be sick."

Jason nodded, but he didn't mean it. He was tired of taking pills. He was tired of being an Attention Deficit kid. No junk food and early bedtimes were boring. It was time for a change—a big change.

Jason tiptoed to the kitchen. He glanced over his shoulder. Was his mother watching? Could she hear him lift the candy-box lid?

The glorious smell greeted his nose. Ah yes! Jason's taste buds started to jig. They

danced the chocolate twist, followed by the ooey-gooey chocolate boogie.

The fantastic smell floating out of the valentine box grabbed Jason. It made him pick out the juiciest mound of chocolate. It made him plop that mound into his mouth.

"Jason Birchall!"

He jumped half out of his skin. Slowly, he turned around. There stood his mother. She glared at him, her hands on her hips.

Jason gulped.

TWO

J ason nearly choked. *She must have come in during the chocolate boogie*, he thought, shutting the box.

He tried to speak. "Yesh?" The heavenly ball of chocolate crowded his mouth.

His mother scolded, "I can't turn my back for one second!"

Jason swallowed. The sweet mound of heaven slid down his throat. Five seconds was too short to enjoy a valentine chocolate.

"Well, Jason?" his mother asked.

"I'm sorry." But Jason was only sorry about one thing—the short time the chocolate had stayed in his mouth.

Mrs. Birchall opened the lid. The smells leaped out of the box. She counted the chocolates. "How many did you eat?"

"Just one."

She stared at the heart-shaped candy box, then at Jason. "Are you sure?"

Jason nodded.

"You *know* what sweets do to you."

But Jason didn't care about being wound up and hyper. He could think of only one thing: dark, rich chocolate.

His mother snatched up the pink valentine box. "I'll put this away." And she carried it out of the kitchen.

Jason peeked around the corner. He watched her turn into the master bedroom. He heard the closet door squeak open.

Good! Jason could almost see the hiding place. It was the same spot where his parents hid Christmas candy. And caramel corn. And Dad's M&M's.

Just then, the garage door opened. Jason ran to meet his dad.

"Here's an early Valentine's day gift," his dad said. He handed the gift to Jason.

Jason tore the wrapping off and looked at

the present. It was a small marker board with a green marker.

"Like it?" his dad asked, smiling.

"Uh, sure, thanks." Jason stared at the gift. *Just what I always wanted,* he thought.

"You can write important things on it," Dad explained. "It will help you remember to take your pills while we're gone."

Jason pulled the green marker off the Velcro. He wrote his name on the board. His stomach felt tight. He gritted his teeth. His parents were no fun. No fun at all! Why did God make parents, anyway?

Jason followed his dad into the house. He shuffled down the hall to his room. Closing the door, he plopped down onto his bean-bag chair.

Jason drew a picture on his new marker board. It was a giant ice cream sundae covered with chocolate candies. And gobs of whipped cream.

He daydreamed about the chocolates in his mother's closet. He thought about his plan. Soon, he wouldn't have to daydream about chocolates. He would gobble them right down!

Jason took off his glasses and twirled them. He danced a wild jig. Friday—two days away. He would trick his grandma. Easy!

Three

At last, it was Friday.

Jason walked home with the other Cul-de-Sac Kids. All the kids lived on Blossom Hill Lane. Seven houses on one cul-de-sac.

"My grandma is spending the weekend," Jason told his friend Dunkum.

"Sounds like fun," Dunkum said.

"No kidding!" Jason said.

Dunkum stopped in the middle of the street and stared at Jason. "What's *that* supposed to mean?"

"Nothin' much." Jason ran and slid on the snow.

Abby Hunter tossed her scarf around her neck. "I think Jason is up to something!"

Dunkum nodded. "I better have a talk with Jason's grandma."

Dee Dee Winters giggled. So did her best friend, Carly Hunter—Abby's little sister. "I *like* your grandma," said Dee Dee.

"Me too," said Carly.

Stacy Henry laughed. "Who needs a sitter when you're in third grade? I stay by myself every day after school."

"But what about for a whole weekend?" Abby asked.

"Guess you're right," Stacy said. "That's too long to be alone."

Abby's Korean brother, Shawn, threw a snowball at Stacy. It bounced off her backpack.

"Why, you!" Stacy dropped her stuff and reached down. She pushed a pile of snow together. "This is war!" she shouted, giggling.

Eric Hagel grinned. "You're in for it now, Shawn!"

The kids watched Stacy smooth out her snowball. She added more snow to it, then patted it hard. She tried to pick it up. It was too heavy.

Shawn marched into the snowy street. "I

help you, Stacy. This make good snowman." He spoke in broken English because he'd just come to the United States. Shawn and his brother, Jimmy, had been adopted by Abby's parents.

"Goody!" shouted Carly. "Let's build a snowman."

"How about a snow monster?" Eric suggested. "The biggest one in the world."

"Make him an alien!" yelled Jason.

"There's no such thing," Abby said.

"So what?" said Jason. "There aren't any monsters, either." But he thought about his plan to trick his grandma. Now, *that* was something a monster might do!

The kids took their school stuff home and came back with buckets of warm water.

"Let's make him in *my* yard!" Jason hollered.

Just then, Grandma Birchall stepped outside. She stood on the porch, waving to Jason.

Jason looked the other way on purpose. He knew what she wanted. It was time for his medicine.

"Jason, dear," she called.

"In a minute," Jason snapped. Then he ran

to help Eric and Dunkum roll up a huge snowball. They grunted as they pushed it across the yard.

Abby and Stacy made a medium-sized ball.

Dee Dee and Carly made the head. Carly started laughing.

"What's so funny?" Abby asked.

Carly kept giggling. "We could call the snow creature Dino Dunce. And give him a walnut-sized brain."

"I know! He could have a tiny head like a Stegosaurus," Dee Dee added.

Eric laughed. "Who said anything about making a dinosaur?"

"Yeah," said Jason. "What happened to our alien?"

"Let's mix him all up," suggested Dunkum.

"Yes!" Shawn shouted. "We make snowman-monster-dino-alien."

"And let's call him our February Snow Creature," said Abby.

"Our what?" Stacy asked.

"You know, like at the St. Paul Winter Carnival in Minnesota," Abby said. "My grandparents took us to see it once."

"Yes!" said Shawn. "We make great snow

creature." He and Jimmy, his little brother, were grinning.

Jason couldn't remember seeing Shawn and Jimmy so excited. Except for the day they learned Abby and Carly's parents were going to adopt them. That was Thanksgiving—three months ago.

Jason had an idea. "We could rope off the cul-de-sac and charge a fee to see our snow creature."

"How much?" Dunkum asked.

"Enough for an ice cream party," yelled Jason.

"You're not supposed to have sweets," Dee Dee reminded him. She wrinkled up her nose.

Jason gritted his teeth. He'd have sweets if he wanted to. He was thinking of his mother's valentine chocolates this very minute.

Jason turned and looked toward his house. *Good!* Grandma had gone inside. *She's probably making supper,* he thought. *Now is a good time to sneak inside. Nothing can stop me now!*

Four

J ason crept onto the porch and tiptoed inside. Grandma was tinkering around in the kitchen. All clear!

He sneaked down the hall and dashed into his parents' bedroom.

Squeak! He slid open the closet.

There were purses and shoe boxes on his mother's side of the closet. Color coded, as always. Red was for dress up. Blue was for work at her beauty shop. Green was for around the house. Everything was in order.

Now for the candy!

Jason pushed his father's shirts aside. Behind them was a shelf for belts and ties and things.

Before he could see the box, Jason smelled

the chocolates. His taste buds shivered. They quivered.

Dark, rich chocolate balls! Waiting to melt into pools of sweet bliss in his mouth.

He reached for the box and opened it. The fattest candy seemed to call his name. Jason placed it on the end of his tongue.

"Gotcha!"

Jason whirled around. He stared into Abby Hunter's face.

"Spit it out!" she said.

"You cwavy?" Jason said, his mouth full.

Abby shook her head. "Say what you want, but we need those outside." She was giggling now as she grabbed the candy box. She held up two plump, juicy chocolates. "What *beautiful* eyes you have!"

Jason stared at his friend. He couldn't believe it. She was going to use his mother's chocolates for the snow creature's eyeballs!

Jason chewed up the gooey candy and swallowed.

Abby waved her finger at him. "Does your grandma know what you just ate?"

"Do I look *that* dumb?" Jason said.

Abby raised her eyebrows. Then she turned

and ran out of the house. But Jason was right behind her.

"Jason, is that you, dear?" It was his grandma calling from the kitchen.

Oops! Jason froze in his tracks. "Uh, yes, Grandma."

She came into the living room wearing an apron. It was tied in a bow around her trim waist. "Come here, dear. I need a hug." She held out her arms.

Jason hugged her but held his breath so she wouldn't smell the chocolate.

"It's time for your medicine, young man." She pulled a bottle of pills out of her pocket. Opening the lid, she put one in Jason's hand.

Jason spun around and hurried out the door.

Grandma called after him, "Do you want a glass of water, dear?"

"Not this time," Jason yelled. And as soon as she wasn't looking, he dropped the pill into the snow. *Poof!* It disappeared.

There! Grown-ups can't tell me what to do! Jason decided. He felt mighty good about taking charge of things. His way.

Five

J ason helped Shawn and Jimmy pour water on the snow. They rubbed out the bumps so the snow would harden nice and smooth.

Jimmy found an old twig and snapped it in two. "Snow Creature . . . funny arms," he said.

Stacy found another twig. "Here, this girl needs three arms."

"*Girl?*" shouted Jason.

Stacy grinned.

Dunkum frowned. He plopped his blue hat on Snow Creature. "There, now it's a *boy!*"

Dee Dee ran home and came back with two pieces of lettuce for ears.

Abby licked the pieces of chocolate. *Smack!* She stuck them on Snow Creature's face.

Jason gritted his teeth. *What a waste!*

The kids clapped. It was perfect, except for one thing. The nose.

"Is *she* a snooty snow creature?" asked Stacy, looking down her own nose.

"No, *he* needs an antenna nose," announced Eric.

"Let's have a nose vote," said Abby. "How many want Stacy's idea?"

Stacy, Dee Dee, Carly, Abby . . . and little Jimmy voted yes.

"No fair!" Jason whined. "Jimmy can't vote with the girls."

Dunkum whistled. "Here's a freaky idea. We'll give S.C. two faces, one on each side of his head."

"S.C.?" asked little Jimmy. He looked confused.

"Santa Claus, right?" Jason said, laughing. The boys cheered.

"Hey, wait a minute," said Abby. "Don't get Jimmy all mixed up. S.C. stands for Snow Creature."

"S.C. need two heads," Jimmy said.

"Yes!" Shawn said. He began rolling up another snowball.

"A two-headed snow creature," said Stacy. "One for the boys; one for the girls!"

"Ours will look beautiful," bragged Dee Dee.

Eric strutted around Snow Creature. "But ours will be better!"

Abby frowned. "This isn't a contest. We're the Cul-de-Sac Kids—we stick together, remember?"

Dunkum grinned. He marched up to Abby and stood beside her. "The president of the cul-de-sac is right."

So the kids set to work, for the fun of it. And by dark, Snow Creature was finished.

The head created by the boys wore Dunkum's blue knit hat. Black olives made the eyes. And a red rubber band formed the mouth.

The head created by the girls wore Abby's straw hat. Red licorice formed the mouth. And lettuce made the ears. Two chocolate eyeballs stared straight at Jason's house.

Jason wished the chocolates were melting in his mouth. Instead of freezing rock hard outside.

"Time for supper," Grandma Birchall called.

Jason hurried to the front porch. He turned to look at Snow Creature once more. *He* was terrific!

Inside, Jason smelled Grandma's meatloaf and potatoes. He ate some of everything. Grandma smiled when he finished.

Boy, did I fool her! She thinks I'm full, Jason thought as he planned his dessert. Ah, dessert! The rest of the valentine chocolates, of course.

The truth was, he shouldn't have chocolate at all. And he knew it. Chocolate made him very hyper, sometimes sick.

Grandma stacked the dishes on the counter while Jason went to the living room. He sat on the sofa waiting for his big chance. Dessert was calling.

Click! Jason turned on the TV with the remote control. He found channel 7 and leaned back. It was a loud, shoot-'em-up cop show.

Grandma peeked around the corner. "Is that something your parents let you watch?" she asked.

"Every night."

"Jason, are you sure?"

"Uh-huh," Jason lied.

At the commercial, Grandma came in with a cup of coffee. Quickly, Jason switched to the news channel.

Grandma settled into a comfortable chair and watched. "This looks interesting," she said, sipping her coffee.

Jason stared at the coffee in Grandma's cup. The dark color reminded him of valentine chocolates—the ones in his mother's closet!

Grandma seemed interested in the local news. So Jason sneaked out of the living room and made a beeline for the hallway.

It was now or never!

Six

Jason found the valentine box and stuffed it under his shirt. He dashed across the hall to his room.

Whoosh! He slid under his bed on his stomach. Grandma would never find him here. Under the bed, he opened the lid. One after another, he ate the chocolates. Mm-m! It was chocolate heaven at last.

After the sixth one, Jason's taste buds rolled over and played dead. He couldn't taste a thing!

Then something strange began to happen. Jason felt shaky all over. Like he could jump up and down and never stop!

He tried to get out from under the bed, but he bumped his head on the box springs.

He tried to slide out backward. His foot was stuck in the bed frame coils. He rocked back and forth.

Crash! His head hit the bed. "Ouch!" he yelled. Jason was trapped. But he couldn't lie still. Inside, his whole body wanted to move. Like tiny grasshoppers dancing and twitching.

He pushed the valentine box aside. *No more, no thanks!*

Now Grandma was calling. Jason stared at the half-eaten candy box. The ooey-gooey chocolates smelled horrible. Besides that, he had a stomachache.

Jason was in big trouble. He hadn't taken his afternoon pill—the pill that helped calm him down. His body needed that medicine.

"Jason," his grandma called again.

"I'm here," whispered Jason, still under the bed.

He was too sick to shout.

"Jason, I dished up some fruit for dessert."

He pushed away from the box springs, trying to get his foot unstuck. He rocked. He rolled. He wiggled.

Bam! The bed frame came loose on one side. It fell on top of him.

"Help!" It was easy to scream now. Jason kept howling till Grandma showed up.

"Goodness! Oh, my dear!" Grandma lifted the bed frame off poor, sick Jason.

Free at last, Jason jumped up. "You saved me. I could've been framed forever."

Grandma scratched her misty gray head. "Are you all right?" Then her eyes grew narrow. She studied him. "You're all chocolaty." The smudges on his face told his secret.

Grandma pointed Jason toward the bathroom. "Let's get you washed up, young man."

He plodded off to clean his face. But when he closed the door, he forgot why he was there. That often happened when he didn't take his pills.

Jason pulled a plastic bag down from the cabinet. It was full of cotton balls. One by one, he lined them up in a row on the sink counter top.

Soon, Grandma was knocking on the door. "Are you all right, dear?"

Jason looked in the mirror. Oops! A chocolaty face stared back. Gooey spots smeared his glasses.

"Jason?" Grandma called again.

"Uh, just a minute." He turned on the faucet. It was hot water. Too hot, so he added cold. Swoosh! The water splashed over the sink, onto the floor.

"Jason!" Grandma sounded upset.

"I'll be right out," Jason grumbled. He leaned over the sink and cupped his hands under the faucet. He rubbed them over his face, spreading the chocolate all around.

Just then, another idea struck. Jason plugged up the sink and floated cotton balls in it. Two handfuls of them.

"I'm coming in!" Grandma called. The bathroom door swung wide. "What a mess you've made," she said and began to clean up.

Jason dried his hands on his jeans. Things had gone crazy. But it was still only Friday. *Plenty of time left before Mom and Dad come home,* he thought.

Friday night! Monster movie night! Jason was dying to see a monster movie. His first ever.

If only he could get rid of the ache in his stomach. If only he could get Grandma to go to bed early!

But how?

Seven

Jason jigged down the hallway to the living room. He plopped into his dad's favorite chair. Holding his stomach, he groaned.

Grandma came in, looking worried. "Let's get some warm tea in you." She touched his arm. "Come in the kitchen, dear."

Jason wasn't paying attention. He reached for the TV section of the paper instead. Something caught his eye. A sale at the pet store—tomorrow!

Jason read the ad. *VALENTINE SPECIAL: FROGS AND LIZARDS, HALF PRICE.*

A frog! For as long as he could remember, Jason had wanted a frog. He would do anything for one.

He dropped the newspaper. "Grandma, can

we go downtown tomorrow?" He turned on the charm. "Please?"

"If you behave yourself, we'll see about it," she said from the kitchen.

Jason burst out laughing. "It's a deal!" But of course, he had no plans to behave. And he would wait to tell Grandma about the frog.

"Your tea is ready," Grandma said.

Jason hurried to the kitchen. "I'll clean up the kitchen for you," he said. Jason wiggled all over waiting for her answer.

"What a dear boy," Grandma said. She pulled out a chair for him. Then she served him a cup of mint tea. Stirring in a little honey, his grandma smiled. "We're having a lovely time together, aren't we?"

Lovely? Jason rubbed his stomach and groaned. "I feel horrible," he said.

"Sip your tea slowly," Grandma said. "It will help."

Jason held his breath and pretended to sip and swallow. "I'm done." He pushed the cup away.

Grandma frowned at him over her glasses. "Perhaps an early bedtime will help."

"After I do the dishes," he said. "And you can watch TV while I do that." He was hoping she'd get sleepy and go to bed early.

"Why, thank you, dear," Grandma said, heading for the living room.

Jason turned on the water at the sink. Next came dish soap. He squeezed out too much, and it made tons of bubbles. Soon, they were dripping down the sides of the counter. And onto the floor.

Jason was getting more and more hyper. His last pill had been at breakfast. His mother had placed it beside his hot oatmeal and toast. Right in front of his nose.

When Jason finished in the kitchen, it was messier than when he started. He held his stomach as he went to his room. *It's too early to go to bed,* he thought.

Peering out the window, he saw lights across the street. Abby and Carly Hunter and their brothers were still up. And Dunkum's lights were on next door. Stacy Henry's, too.

"All the Cul-de-Sac Kids are up," he muttered. "It's only 7:30." Shoving the curtains closed, he planned his next move.

He hopped like a frog over to his closet and pulled out his robe and pajamas.

"Ribbit!" he croaked over and over. Then he got undressed.

His plan was perfect! Now if he could just stay awake till Grandma went to bed.

Eight

Grandma tucked Jason in and gave him a kiss on the forehead. "Sleep well, dear," she said.

"Good night, Grandma," he whispered, pretending to be tired.

"I think I'll read awhile. It's early. If you need anything, I'll be across the hall in your parents' room."

"Thanks, Grandma." Jason wanted to sound polite. More than that, he wanted to trick his grandma. Late-night TV was on his mind. Once she was asleep, he would get up.

Jason listened to the clock in the hall. He counted the ticks, but he couldn't lie still.

At last, he sat up in bed. Was Grandma asleep yet?

Tiptoeing across the hall, Jason peeked into the room. His grandma was sitting up in bed, but her eyes were shut. And a book lay open on her lap.

Yes! Jason closed her door softly and dashed to the living room. He lay on the floor in front of the TV. Some scary show was on. He could tell by the music.

Jason gritted his teeth as a giant snowman roared down from the mountain. It had a monster face.

A snow creature? thought Jason. *Nah, couldn't be.*

Suddenly, the music changed. It got louder and higher in pitch. Jason turned down the volume. He didn't want Grandma to wake up.

Phooey on grown-ups! thought Jason.

He sat close to the TV. The giant snowman clumped down the mountain and across the field. It was heading straight for two boys. They were shoveling snow.

Jason watched, eyes glued to the screen. What was the snow giant going to do? Why didn't the boys turn and run?

Jason held his breath. *Yikes!* His stomach knotted up as the snow giant crept behind the boys.

Leaping up, Jason stood in the middle of the living room. The snow giant roared and the boys ran for their lives. Jason's muscles felt frozen. His breath came in short puffs as he watched the boys run. Jason wished they'd hurry. The snow giant was catching up with them.

"Hurry! Get away," Jason said to the TV.

Just then—*cre-eak!*—Jason's front door inched open.

Jason jerked around, ready to fight off the snow monster. *"No!"* he yelled as a furry hand touched the doorknob.

Jason's heart did a giant flip.

Nine

"Anybody home?" It was Dunkum. He stomped his feet on the mat. "It's freezing out there."

"Don't you ever knock?" Jason asked.

"I did," Dunkum insisted.

"I didn't hear you," Jason replied. He pointed to the TV screen. "Watch this."

Dunkum sat on the sofa for a minute. Then he frowned. "I don't watch scary stuff."

Jason wasn't listening now. He was watching the snow giant bend the boys' shovels in half.

During the commercial, Jason stretched. "What are you doing here?" he asked Dunkum.

Dunkum grinned. "I'm checking up on you."

"I'm fine," Jason said.

Dunkum got up and looked in the kitchen. "It's a mess in there. Where's your grandma?"

"What do you care?"

Dunkum frowned. "You can't fool me, Jason Birchall." He pulled something out of his pocket. "Look what I found in the snow."

Jason stared at it. It was his afternoon medicine. The pill he should have taken. "Hey, where did you get that?"

"From the pill fairy," Dunkum teased.

Jason held his hands up like a boxer.

Dunkum dodged Jason's swing. "Whatcha doin' Sunday morning?" Dunkum asked.

"Me?"

"You and your grandma," Dunkum said.

"Not much," Jason said.

"Why don't you come to church? There's room in Abby's van." Dunkum turned to leave.

Jason remembered the Christmas service at Dunkum and Abby's church. The ushers had given out candy. Maybe they'd have valentine candy *this* Sunday!

"Sure, I'll come," Jason replied.

"Good." Dunkum's eyes sparkled. "It's a special day. We're having a kids' choir."

Jason liked music. It made him want to dance. Slow or fast, it didn't matter. "That's good," he said, but the commercial was over now. And the snow giant was back.

Jason hardly heard his friend say good-bye.

At the next commercial, Jason tiptoed to his room. He pulled the chocolates out from under his bed. Time for a little snack.

By the end of the movie, Jason wished Dunkum had stayed. They could have shivered together with fear. But Dunkum was smart. He didn't watch this stuff.

It was late, and Jason was wiped out. He jumped into bed without washing his face or brushing his teeth. He held his stomach. It was hurting again. But not as bad as the pain in his head.

He shook all over and scooted under his covers. Jason glanced at his clock. The time glowed back at him. It was past midnight!

The room was darker than usual. It made Jason nervous. If he stared into the blackness long enough, little snow creatures began to appear.

Eek! Jason hid under the covers. But he

couldn't hide from the snow giant's roar. The sound was stuck in his brain. It made him quiver and quake.

Suddenly, Jason heard another sound. Low at first. Then it grew louder. He reached for the light. Dashing to the window, Jason cupped his hands on the frosty glass.

The two-headed snow creature shimmered under the streetlight. One set of eyes stared back at him—the chocolate ones.

Jason bumped his head on the window. He blinked. "What's going on?" he whispered.

Snow Creature moved his twig arms.

Jason rubbed his eyes.

Then it happened again!

Thump! Thump! Jason's heart pounded in his ears. *Has Snow Creature come to life?*

Ten

Whoosh! Jason closed the curtains. "Grandma!" he hollered.

She rushed into the room. "What is it, dear?"

Jason danced around, trying to tell her what he'd seen. "It started with a low roar. I looked out the window. That's when I saw him move!"

"Please slow down, Jason. What are you saying?"

"It's Snow Creature. He's alive! Look outside!"

A sleepy smile spread across her face. "You must be dreaming."

Jason tugged on her nightgown. "Come see for yourself."

"You can't see anything outside with this light on." She flipped the switch off.

Jason stood at the window. "Just watch," he whispered.

The two of them waited. And waited. The snow creature stood very still.

At last, Grandma tucked Jason in bed again. "It must be all those chocolates you ate," she said. And she blew a kiss.

Jason shook all over. There was a live snow creature out there making roaring sounds, just like in the movie. And Grandma was going back to bed!

Not Jason. He reached for a book from his shelf. It was a Christmas gift from Abby Hunter. It had a Bible verse and a story for each day of the year.

Jason pulled his knees up to his chin and read: *Children, obey your parents in the Lord, for this is right. Honor your father and mother . . . that it may go well with you and that you may enjoy long life on the earth.*

Jason stopped reading. He thought about things going well if he obeyed his parents. He wanted to live a long time on the earth. And he thought about obeying. *That* was hard.

Next, he read the story. It was so good, he forgot about being scared. The book from Abby had done the trick. Nothing could scare him now. He turned the light out and fell asleep.

■■■

Hours later, Jason heard a noise at his window. He sat up in bed. There it was again.

Someone was knocking on his bedroom window!

Jason was too tired to care. Maybe he was dreaming. He hoped so. Then he could snuggle down into his blankets again.

Scr-i-i-tch! Scr-a-a-tch!

Jason leaped out of bed. He peeked between the curtains. His heart jumped.

Snow Creature was staring into his window. He had walked all the way across the yard!

Jason dashed away from the window, yelling for Grandma. She *had* to believe him now. Jason raced across the hall. Running up to the bed, he pulled the covers down. The bed was empty!

Jason ran out of the room and down the hall. "Grandma!" he called.

He opened the front door and ran out into the night. He looked around. Snow Creature was still standing beside his window.

Jason darted back inside and slammed the door. His heart thumped wildly.

Suddenly, he had an idea. He would go outside and tell off Snow Creature! Who did he think he was, scaring him like that?

Jason pulled his coat on over his pajamas. He shook with fright. What if Snow Creature had gotten to Grandma's room first? What if he had taken her away?

Jason ran through the house, shouting, "Grandma, where are you?"

But Grandma was nowhere to be found!

Eleven

At that moment, Jason missed the grown-ups in his life. His dad, his mom, and his grandma . . . all of them. He was on his own now. Alone with scary Snow Creature!

He took a deep breath and opened the front door. He stared at Snow Creature. A mean look shot out of the icy monster's eyes. Jason shivered.

And then it happened. A low roar bellowed out of Snow Creature's mouth.

Yikes! Jason wanted to run inside. But no! He was determined to be brave. Marching up to Snow Creature, Jason punched his snowy stomach.

"You're not alive," Jason shouted. "This must be a bad dream."

Snow Creature took a giant leap toward him.

But Jason stood still. "All I have to do is pinch myself, and you'll be back where you belong," he shouted. He pointed to the spot where he and the Cul-de-Sac Kids had made the creature.

"That's what *you* think," Snow Creature thundered, reaching out to grab Jason. "Your grandmother is mine now. And you are next!"

"No!" screamed Jason. He twisted away from Snow Creature's reach. "No!"

■ ■ ■

"Jason, dear! Wake up! It's Grandma."

He twisted and rolled around in his sheets.

"You're dreaming," Grandma said.

Jason opened his eyes. The sweetest wrinkled face in the world smiled down at him. He rubbed his eyes. "Nobody should watch scary shows," Jason whispered. "Not ever."

His grandma nodded slowly. "It's almost time for breakfast," she said. "And your pill."

Jason started to groan but stopped.

"Maybe you won't have to take pills when you're a grown-up," she said.

Grown-up, thought Jason. *A nice word.*

Grandma went to fix scrambled eggs and toast. Jason could almost taste it. A good breakfast beat chocolate candy any day!

At the table, Jason took his pill. And after breakfast, he brushed his teeth and washed his face.

Jason went to his room and wrote on his marker board.

Always remember—

1. *Take pills*
2. *Watch good TV shows*
3. *Go to bed early*
4. *Obey grown-ups (like parents and grand-parents)*

Jason spotted the book from Abby. He remembered the verse about obeying parents. Then, kneeling beside his bed, Jason talked to God. He was sorry about watching the scary movie. And about eating his mother's chocolates. He was sorry about not wanting any grown-ups around.

After the prayer, Jason hopped around his

room like a frog. He pretended his bed was a lily pond.

When Grandma peeked in, he shouted, "Ribbit! Forgive it?"

She came in and stood beside the bed. "That's an interesting word."

"Oh, Grandma, I'm sorry I didn't obey you. I got out of bed and watched a scary monster movie and . . ."

"I know you did, dear," she said calmly.

"You do?"

Grandma nodded. "You didn't expect me to sleep through all that roaring, did you?"

Jason grinned. He should have known. "Well, I'm sorry. And that's the truth."

"It was a hard lesson," Grandma said. "And goodness me, what scary music!" She put her hand to her forehead.

Jason gave her a big squeeze. "Oh, Grandma, I love you!"

■ ■ ■

Later that night, Jason fell asleep thinking about his visit to the pet shop. And his half-priced frog—a valentine gift from Grandma.

But when he dreamed, it wasn't about frogs. Or scary snow monsters. It was about grown-ups. Grown-ups like his mom and dad.

And tomorrow, they were coming home!

BOOK 5

Frog Power

To
Shanna Dreuth,
who likes slimy things.
Once she caught twelve frogs
and carried them in her pockets all day.

One

Stacy Henry was late for school. It was the first time all year. But Stacy couldn't help it.

Today was Pet Day for Miss Hershey's third-grade class. And something slimy and green was coming to Blossom Hill School. Jason Birchall said so.

Stacy tiptoed down the hall carrying her cockapoo puppy. She stopped at the classroom door and peeked inside. Her classmates were showing off their pets.

Abby Hunter, Stacy's best friend, was cuddling Snow White, a fluffy white dog. Shawn Hunter, Abby's adopted Korean brother, was tickling Snow White's ears.

Stacy spotted Dunkum in the corner of the room. His real name was Edward Mifflin, but no one called him that. He was Dunkum, the tallest and the best basketball player in school.

Dunkum lifted Blinkee, his fat gray rabbit, out of the cage. He set her on his desk. Stepping back, he clapped his hands two times. Blinkee sat up on her haunches and wiggled her pink little nose. She was the cutest rabbit Stacy had ever seen.

Just then, a low croaking sound came from the middle of the classroom. Blinkee pricked up her long bunny ears.

Stacy shivered. She hid behind the classroom door. The croaking sound continued. *The slimy green nightmare is here! Jason Birchall's bullfrog is the worst creature God ever made,* she decided.

Stacy sneaked around the door and stared across the room. A glass aquarium sat on the desk behind hers. Inches from her desk was Jason's bullfrog. On top of its head, two eyes bulged out.

Stacy leaned against the classroom door, wishing she could go home. She put Sunday

Funnies, her cockapoo, on the floor. He strained on his leash.

Abby and Shawn ran to Jason's desk to see the noisy bullfrog. Dunkum carried his rabbit over for a look. Soon, most of the class had gathered around the ten-gallon glass tank.

But not Stacy. She took a deep breath and crept to Miss Hershey's desk. Sunday Funnies followed on his leash.

The teacher smiled at her. "You're a little late today." She petted Sunday Funnies' head.

"I almost didn't come," Stacy blurted out.

Her teacher frowned. "I'm sorry to hear that, Stacy. Are you feeling all right?"

"I'm not sick or anything." Stacy glanced over her shoulder. *Icksville! Why did Miss Hershey have to change the desks around yesterday?*

"Stacy? Is something wrong?" the teacher asked.

Stacy turned around slowly. "I, uh . . . no, I'm fine, thanks." Stacy inched toward her desk, past Eric Hagel.

Eric's hamster was nibbling on a piece of carrot inside his cage.

"Nice hamster," Stacy said. She hardly even looked at the hamster. Instead, she stared at Jason's bullfrog at the end of the row.

Eric coughed. "Earth to Stacy! Guess what I named my hamster?"

"I don't know," Stacy muttered. She was thinking about a slimy bullfrog named Croaker.

"Come on, just guess," Eric insisted.

"Uh . . . Slimy?" It was a silly name for a hamster, but Stacy couldn't get the horrible green bullfrog off her mind.

"Not even close," Eric said.

"Then I give up," Stacy said flatly. The hamster made her sneeze.

"This is the smartest hamster in the world," Eric bragged. "Her name is Fran the Ham. And does she ever ham it up!" He laughed. "Get it—*ham* it up?"

"Of course I get it," Stacy snapped. And she clumped off to her desk wishing, wishing. She wished Jason Birchall would take Croaker home.

Shawn Hunter rushed over to Stacy's desk. He grinned. "I rub Sunday Funnies' neck, yes?"

Stacy nodded. "He likes you, Shawn. Ever

since the day he got hit by a car and you helped him."

Shawn's eyes danced as he stroked the cockapoo.

Dunkum put his rabbit on the floor beside Sunday Funnies. The rabbit and the cockapoo sniffed each other. Sunday Funnies wagged his curly puff of a tail.

"I think they like each other," Dunkum said.

Stacy petted the rabbit. Her eyes began to water. She sneezed three times.

Miss Hershey asked everyone to sit down. "We have an exciting day ahead of us, class." She grinned. Everyone knew Miss Hershey loved animals.

Stacy grabbed a tissue from inside her desk and blew her nose. Then she put Sunday Funnies in her lap and cuddled him. "It's a good thing *you* don't make me sneeze," she whispered to him.

Suddenly, Jason Birchall reached over his desk. He was petting Sunday Funnies' head.

Stacy pulled her pet away.

Jason frowned. "What's the matter with you?"

"Stay away from him," Stacy said. Gently, she put her puppy on the floor and sat down. She slid her chair close to her desk. Far away from Jason's creepy bullfrog.

Her stomach was squished against the desk. But it was better than having frog breath in her hair!

Two

Miss Hershey called roll. Then the kids began to show off their pets.

Eric Hagel lugged his hamster cage to the front of the room. Ker-plop! He set it down on Miss Hershey's desk. "Meet my hamster, Fran the Ham."

The class giggled.

Eric continued. "Fran likes parade music." He grinned. "She likes 'Stars and Stripes Forever.'"

Miss Hershey sat at her desk. She leaned on her elbows and peered into the hamster cage. "Does Fran do any tricks?" she asked.

Eric put his hands on his hips. "How many want to see Fran do her amazing routine?"

Everyone cheered.

"First, I have to get the music ready."

Jason groaned.

Turning around, Stacy muttered, "What's the matter? Isn't *Croaker* smart enough to do tricks?"

Jason shot her his best cross-eyes.

"Frog eyes," Stacy whispered.

Jason made another face.

Just then, the beat of drums filled the room. Brassy trumpets and trombones joined in.

Stacy couldn't believe it. Fran the Ham was running on a little turn wheel. Faster and faster! Fran's tiny hamster feet were flying.

"Now check this out," Eric told the class. He pushed stop on his MP3 player.

Fran the Ham slowed down. She stopped!

The kids clapped with delight. Eric carried the hamster cage back to his seat.

Stacy pulled out a pencil and wrote a note.

Dear Eric,
I really do like your hamster. She is very smart. I'm sorry I didn't believe you.

Your friend,
Stacy

Stacy folded the note. She felt good about it. Eric was her neighbor on Blossom Hill Lane—their cul-de-sac. *And the Cul-de-Sac Kids stick together, no matter what,* she remembered. That's the way it was.

Stacy put the note in her jeans pocket. She would give the note to Eric at recess.

Miss Hershey called Shawn Hunter next.

Abby raised her hand. "Shawn and I want to show our dog together. Is that OK?"

Miss Hershey nodded.

Shawn led Snow White to the front of the room.

Abby followed, carrying a bag of doggie treats. "Shawn will introduce our dog," she said.

Shawn's dark eyes shone. "Snow White is Shih Tzu puppy," he said. "Her family go back very long time—to Chinese courts. Long ago, this kind of dog was royal pet."

Abby took off Snow White's leash. "Now Snow White will do some tricks for you," she announced.

Abby moved her arm in circles without saying a word. Snow White rolled over three times. Abby gave her a treat. Snow White chomped it right down.

Next, Snow White played dead. The class called out her name. Jason hopped out of his seat and tickled Snow White's ear. The dog didn't budge an inch!

At last, Shawn snapped his fingers. Snow White leaped up for another treat.

The kids clapped loudly.

Abby and Shawn took their seats. Snow White sat on the floor near Shawn's desk.

Miss Hershey checked her record book. "Jason Birchall, you're next."

When Jason stood up, Stacy scooted down in her seat. Far away from the bullfrog behind her.

The glass cage was too heavy to move. So Jason was going to show off Croaker from his desk.

Stacy peeked around her chair.

Whoosh! Jason took off the wood frame. A silly grin stretched across his face. Then he reached inside.

Stacy shivered as Jason's hands caught the slimy green bullfrog.

Icksville! She covered her eyes.

Three

Jason held his frog high. "This is Croaker." He pointed to the round spots behind the frog's eyes. "These are Croaker's ears. He can hear sounds underwater."

Jason pranced around his desk. Even with his medicine, he was still hyper sometimes. Up and down the row he paced, showing off his bullfrog.

Some of the kids were brave and touched Croaker's skin. When Jason stopped at Abby Hunter's desk, she stuck her pointer finger out. Then she closed her eyes, wrinkled her nose, and touched him. Her eyes popped open. "Ew!"

Jason skipped up to Stacy's desk. "It's *your* turn." He held the frog in front of her face.

What's it feel like? Stacy wondered. She stared at the frog. "I pass," she said, sliding back in her seat.

Jason grinned. "You sure?"

"Uh-huh." Stacy looked into the giant eyes of the bullfrog. She felt sick.

Quick as a flash, Croaker leaped out of Jason's hands . . . and into Stacy's lap!

"Get it off me!" she screamed. Her fingers bumped against the bullfrog's skin. "Ick!"

Before Jason could grab him, Croaker jumped off Stacy's lap and landed on Dunkum's desk.

"I catch! I catch!" Shawn cried in broken English. Letting go of Snow White's leash, Shawn dashed after Croaker. Then Snow White darted after Shawn, barking loudly.

Soon . . .

Sunday Funnies was yipping.

Fran the Ham was twittering.

Croaker was croaking.

Cats were meowing.

A parrot was screeching.

But Miss Hershey was silent. She simply sat at her desk and smiled.

After chasing the frog around the room two

more times, Jason caught Croaker. He put him back in the cage and closed the wooden lid. "There," said Jason. "I think he needs my ADD medicine."

Eric laughed. So did the other boys.

Stacy didn't think it was funny. She raised her hand. "May I be excused, please?"

Miss Hershey nodded.

Stacy dashed out of the classroom and down the hall. It was time to get rid of the froggy feel on her hands.

The girls' room was empty. *Good*, she thought. Filling her hands with liquid soap, Stacy scrubbed and rubbed and scrubbed some more.

Suddenly, Stacy heard a strange sound. It was coming from the stall behind her. She listened. *What on earth?* She dried her hands and waited.

There it was again. It sounded like . . .

Out from under the door scampered her puppy.

"Sunday Funnies!" she cried. "*What* are you doing?"

The puppy's head was dripping wet.

"Oh, you're thirsty, is that it?" Stacy shook

her finger at him. "Toilets are not for drinking." And she went into the stall to check.

Thank goodness, the toilet was flushed! Stacy lathered up her hands with soap and washed Sunday Funnies' head and face.

Then she held him up to the dryer.

Minutes later, Miss Hershey came in. "Are you all right, Stacy?"

Stacy nodded. "Everything's under control . . . now."

Miss Hershey touched Stacy's shoulder. "Let's get you back to class. I think you'll like the story today."

Stacy followed Miss Hershey down the hall. She wanted to forget about Jason's bullfrog. Forever.

"We're reading 'The Frog Prince,'" Miss Hershey said as she opened the classroom door.

Stacy dragged her feet. She felt worse than ever. It was bad enough having a frog breathe down her neck. Now she had to read about one, too!

"Super icksville," she muttered on the way to her desk. *Who wants to read* that *fairy tale?*

She looked at the clock. Fifteen minutes till recess. Fifteen minutes too many!

Four

Once upon a time . . ."

Stacy heard the class reading out loud. She skipped ahead to the pictures. An ugly green frog was in a well, and a princess was crying. She remembered the beginning of the story.

"What's wrong, little princess?" the frog asked.

The princess sobbed, "My beautiful gold necklace has fallen into the well."

"Dry your tears," croaked the frog. "I can help. What will you give me if I find it?"

"Whatever you wish, my dear frog," said the princess.

Stacy wanted to choke. Who ever heard of calling a frog *my dear*?

Finding her place, Stacy continued to read. The frog was doing a good job of tricking the princess. He wanted to have supper with her and drink from her silver cup!

The princess wiped her tears and nodded yes.

"And that's not all I want," the frog said.

The princess looked surprised. "What else?"

"I want to sleep in your fine house."

She looked at the frog. "I know just the place for you. Will you get my golden necklace now?" the princess begged.

"One more thing." The frog's eyes blinked. "I want to be friends."

Stacy slammed the book shut. This was too much!

A low croaking sound made her jump. Jason's bullfrog was at it again.

Stacy spun around. "Keep your frog quiet!" she whispered.

Jason frowned. "He's hungry. Wanna help me catch bugs at recess?"

Bugs!
 Bullfrogs!
  Frog fairy tales!
   What a horrible day!

Stacy watched the second hand on the clock. 5 . . . 4 . . . 3 . . . 2 . . . 1 . . . recess!

The bell rang, and Stacy was the first one outside. She walked Sunday Funnies around the playground on his leash.

Jason and Eric were digging for ants near the sidewalk—probably to feed that slimy old frog. Stacy handed Eric the note she'd written. Then she ran to the swings.

Soon, Abby and her little sister, Carly, came over. Carly was in first grade. She held the leashes for Snow White and Sunday Funnies while the girls swung.

Abby leaned back, pulling hard against the swing. "Do you like 'The Frog Prince' so far?"

"It's OK, I guess," Stacy said.

Abby smiled. "I like the ending best."

"I haven't read the ending yet," Stacy said.

"Why not?" Abby asked.

Stacy shook her head. "It gives me the creeps. My dad was reading the story to me the day he left me and my mom."

Abby twisted her swing and let it spin.

Stacy copied her friend and whirled around.

She could almost hear her dad's voice reading out loud to her. She pushed her sneakers against the sand.

Abby changed the subject. "Let's dye Easter eggs at my house next week."

Stacy didn't want to think about Easter eggs. Another holiday without her dad.

Stacy jumped out of the swing. "I know! Let's do something different this year."

"Like what?" Abby asked. She held the leashes for Snow White and Sunday Funnies so Carly could swing.

"Let's have an Easter pet parade," Stacy shouted.

"Double dabble good idea," Abby said.

"Goody!" Carly said. Her golden curls shone in the sunlight.

"Count the pets in the cul-de-sac," Stacy said.

"Let's see. There's Snow White and Sunday Funnies," said Abby.

"Don't forget our baby ducks, Quacker and Jack," Carly said, swinging higher. "One belongs to Jimmy, and one is mine." Jimmy was the younger of Abby and Carly's two Korean brothers.

Abby pulled a tablet and pen out of her jeans pocket. "There's Blinkee, Dunkum's rabbit, and Dee Dee's cat, Mister Whiskers. That makes six."

"And Eric's hamster, Fran the Ham," said Stacy. "That's seven."

"Ribbit!" Carly stopped the swing with her feet. "Don't forget Jason's bullfrog." She giggled and ran to catch up with her friend Dee Dee.

Stacy shivered. No way did she want Croaker in *her* pet parade!

The recess bell rang. "Since we only have a half day today, let's have a meeting after school," Abby said.

"Good idea," Stacy said. And she ran across the playground with her puppy scampering ahead.

The line for Miss Hershey's class was full of kids with pets. Sunday Funnies barked at Jason. Croaker was sitting inside Jason's shirt pocket! Bulging eyes stuck out over the top of his pocket.

Abby laughed. "What's Croaker doing out here?"

"Frogs need exercise, too," Jason explained.

Eric turned around. "Animals need attention, whether they're ugly or not."

Shawn laughed a high-pitched giggle.

But Stacy didn't feel like laughing at all.

Five

Stacy was glad school was out early. She went with Abby to pick up Carly after school. Carly was waiting with Dee Dee Winters beside the first-grade door.

Shawn and Jimmy, Abby's Korean brothers, walked with them across the playground.

Jason's mom picked him up in her car. The frog aquarium was too heavy to carry home.

Soon, Eric came with Fran the Ham, and Dunkum with Blinkee. The Cul-de-Sac Kids always walked together. It was one of Abby's ideas. She was the president of the Cul-de-Sac Kids—nine kids who lived on Blossom Hill Lane.

Carly and Dee Dee held hands as they skipped. Stacy remembered holding hands with Abby when they were in first grade. That had been the year after Stacy's dad moved out.

"Spring is almost here!" Abby shouted.

The sun was warm on Stacy's back. "And then comes summer!" she squealed.

"Yes! School over in two months," Shawn yelled.

Dunkum and Eric had their hands full with cages. One for Blinkee and one for Fran the Ham. Shawn helped Eric carry Fran's.

Just then, Abby turned around in the middle of the cul-de-sac. "Everyone meet at Dunkum's after lunch," she said. "We have important things to discuss."

Carly giggled. "I already know what Abby's gonna say."

"What is meeting about?" little Jimmy asked.

"Come and find out," Dee Dee bossed.

"Abby, you tell now!" Jimmy yelled.

"It's not really a secret," Abby told her brother and all the kids. "But we could surprise our parents for Easter."

"Yes, let's," said Stacy. She couldn't wait for the meeting.

"What surprise?" Jimmy asked.

"Stacy is planning a pet parade," said Abby.

The kids liked the idea. Stacy could tell by the way everyone hurried home for lunch.

She unlocked her front door and went to fix a sandwich. "It's just you and me," she said to Sunday Funnies. She poured dog food into his dish. Standing up, she saw a note stuck to the refrigerator. "What's this?"

Stacy began to read.

Dear Stacy,

Your dad called this morning. He's going to be in town over Easter and wants to see us. We'll talk tonight, OK?

Love you, honey—
Mom

"Listen to this!" Stacy sat down beside her puppy and read the note out loud. She hugged Sunday Funnies. It was a strange name for a dog, but it fit. He could sniff out the Sunday newspaper and find the funny papers. Before anyone else!

A tall paper hat—made from the Sunday

comics—would be the perfect Easter hat for him. Stacy could almost see the cul-de-sac pets marching, hopping, and jumping down Blossom Hill Lane. The pet parade would be the perfect Easter surprise for her dad!

Stacy made a peanut butter and jelly sandwich. She drank a glass of milk with it. Nibbling on an apple, Stacy dashed off to Dunkum's.

She passed Jason's house on the way. Just thinking about Croaker made her shiver. He was the ugliest creature on earth.

Stacy wished Jason's bullfrog would go jump in a well. Then the pet parade would be perfect!

Six

Stacy tossed her sneakers beside the steps in Dunkum's basement. Sitting on the floor, she finished eating her apple.

Dunkum whistled, and the kids got quiet.

Abby plopped down in her president's chair—a blue beanbag. "OK," she began. "Is everyone here?"

The kids looked around.

"Someone's missing," Abby said.

Eric pushed his hair back. "Did we forget to tell Jason?"

"I thought *you* told him," Dunkum said.

Shawn stood up. "I go get Jason."

Stacy felt funny inside.

When Shawn came back with Jason, the Cul-de-Sac Kids began to plan the parade.

"Stacy is a good planner," Abby said. "She should be in charge of arranging the pets."

Dunkum brought a marker board from his father's study. He handed a blue marker to Stacy. "You make a list of all the girl animals." He drew a black line dividing the board in half. "I'll write the boy animals on this side."

Girls	Boys
Quacker—Carly's duck	Jack—Jimmy's duck
Snow White—Shawn's dog	Mr. Whiskers—Dee Dee's cat
Blinkee—Dunkum's rabbit	Sunday Funnies—Stacy's dog
Fran the Ham—Eric's hamster	Croaker—Jason's bullfrog

Stacy turned around. "What about *you*, Abby?"

Shawn leaped off the floor. "Abby play march on speaker."

"Good idea!" Stacy said.

"Or Abby could pull a wagon full of my grandpa's birdcages," Eric suggested. "He has three canaries and two parakeets."

Stacy looked at Abby. "Wanna?"

Abby nodded. "I'll carry the speaker in one hand, and pull the wagon with the other."

"I could buy a *lady* frog for you," Jason said. "Would you like that?"

"Uh . . . that's OK," Stacy said quickly. "Abby is our props manager and bird tamer. Besides, one frog on the block is enough."

Carly and Dee Dee giggled.

"Let's make Easter bonnets for the girl animals," said Stacy. "Who wants to help me make them?"

Abby shot up her hand.

"What about bow ties for the boy animals?" Eric said. "Hey, Stacy, wanna help me?"

Stacy smiled. "OK!"

"Good idea," Jason croaked. "I'll help, too. Ribbit!"

Stacy groaned. Had Eric tricked her into touching Croaker? Again?

Abby ended the meeting. "Remember, don't tell your parents. It's a big surprise. Stacy's head of the parade. She'll make sure all the animals are dressed for the show."

Stacy scrambled for her sneakers. Keeping a secret was not a problem. But tying a bow around a bullfrog's neck? *That* was a problem!

Seven

Stacy ran home to clean her room. Something bugged her about Jason's horrible frog. What was it?

She stood on a chair and dusted the shelf in her closet. In the back, Stacy found her old fairy-tale book.

She jumped off the chair and sat on her bed. Slowly, she turned the pages. It was filled with beautiful pictures. And memories of her dad.

Stacy picked up the bookmark. It had marked the spot in the middle of the story. The one her father was reading to her before he left.

Stacy turned the page. "Oh no!" Staring up from the page was a giant green bullfrog.

The story was "The Frog Prince"—the same one that Stacy was reading for school.

Whoosh! Stacy slammed the book shut. A puff of dust flew out. "I hate this story!" she yelled. "I hate frogs!"

Stacy stomped out of her bedroom and down the hall. It was time to think about Easter bonnets and bow ties. Anything but frogs!

In the living room, Stacy searched through old newspapers. She found the Sunday paper from last week.

Her puppy scampered down the hall. He nosed his way into the comics. He'd found them again!

Stacy held up the color page to her face and sniffed. To her, it didn't smell any different from the other pages. She snuggled her puppy. "How do you do it, you silly?"

Stacy folded the comics page in half and began to make a tall pointed hat. She found scissors and glue in the kitchen. Then she made a bow tie to match.

Stacy giggled as she dressed Sunday Funnies. She picked him up and ran to her room. Standing in front of the long mirror, she held up her cockapoo. "You'll be the star of the Easter parade."

"Woof!" Sunday Funnies agreed.

Stacy heard the garage door rumble. "Mom's home!" She hid the Easter hat and bow tie in her closet. Then she ran to the top of the steps. She couldn't wait to find out more about her dad. Was he *really* coming?

Her mother hugged her close when she came in. "Hi, honey, how was school?"

"OK." She followed her mother into the kitchen.

Her mother sat at the kitchen table. "Whew! I need a vacation."

"Disneyland?" Stacy suggested.

Stacy's mother chuckled. "That's not what I had in mind." She went to the refrigerator. When she opened the door, the note fell off.

Stacy ran to pick up the note. Now was her big chance. "Why is Daddy coming to town?"

"He's coming on business and . . ." Stacy's mother stopped for a second. "He wants to see you."

Stacy held up the note. "This says he wants to see *us*." Stacy hoped that meant something. Maybe Daddy was coming back!

"He's coming Friday afternoon," her mother said.

Three days from now! "Let's invite him for supper," Stacy pleaded.

"Not this time," her mother said.

Stacy left the room. "Not this time," she whispered to herself. "Not this time, and not ever!" Why couldn't her parents at least be friends?

Stacy went to her room and closed the door. She found her storybook. It reminded her of the best days of her life.

"Let's find out what happens to the frog prince," she said to Sunday Funnies.

Happy and sad feelings jumbled up inside her. She found the bookmark and began to read.

Eight

Stacy pretended her father was sitting next to her, reading out loud.

The princess was talking to the frog. "I promise to do everything you said." But the princess secretly hoped the frog would forget. She didn't want a nasty frog coming into the castle! But she said it again, "I promise."

The frog went down, down. Deep into the well. The princess watched and waited.

Up he came with the gold necklace in his mouth. He tossed it onto the grass.

"Oh!" said the princess. "My beautiful necklace!" And she picked it up and ran away.

"Wait a minute!" croaked the frog. "You forgot to take me with you."

But the princess didn't wait for the frog.
She ran all the way to the castle. And soon
she forgot about him.

Stacy stopped reading. *What a horrible
girl,* she thought. *The princess didn't even
say thank you.*

Stacy stared at the picture of the princess.

Knock, knock!

Stacy jumped. "Come in."

It was Abby. She was carrying a white
plastic bag. "Hi, Stacy. What are you doing?"

"Reading." Stacy showed her the book.

"Oh, I like the bright colors," Abby said.
"Where'd you get it?"

"From my dad." Stacy turned to the front
of the book. "It was a birthday present a long
time ago."

Abby smiled. "It's really nice."

Stacy moved over on the bed. "Guess what?"

"You hate Jason's bullfrog, right?"

Stacy felt uneasy. "It's just so . . . uh, so
ugly."

"God made lots of weird-looking animals,"
Abby said. "And my dad thinks God probably
laughs about it sometimes."

Stacy nodded. Abby was lucky to have a

father who loved God—even though it wasn't luck at all.

"My dad's coming for a visit this Friday," Stacy said.

"Double dabble good!" Abby said. "What a fantastic Good Friday present."

"I hope so." Stacy felt the mix of sad and happy feelings again.

Nine

I haven't seen my dad in a long time," Stacy said. "It's a little scary."

"You'll do OK," Abby said softly. "You love him, right?"

Stacy sat up straight. "I'm worried that Mom might get mad."

Abby leaned closer. "Why would she?"

"If I'm nice to my dad, my mom might get upset." Stacy hugged the storybook.

Abby touched Stacy's hand. "Just be yourself. I like you best that way."

"It's not easy sometimes," Stacy replied. "Not around my parents."

Abby raised her eyebrows. "Why not?"

"Because I don't want to hurt either one of

them. Your parents aren't divorced. Maybe you don't understand."

Abby nodded. "You're right. I can't imagine my dad not living with us."

Stacy grabbed Abby's hand. She felt tears slide down her cheek.

Abby bowed her head. "Let's pray, OK?" Abby was like that. She prayed anytime and anywhere.

"Dear Lord," she began. "I don't understand about divorce, but you do. Help Stacy have a good time with her father when he comes." Abby took a deep breath. "And help Stacy remember that Jason's bullfrog is part of your creation. In Jesus' name, amen."

"Amen," Stacy repeated. She felt warm all over.

Abby pulled some tissue paper out of her plastic bag. "Carly and I made hat patterns for all the pets." She held up some tissue paper. Some were little. Some big.

"How cute," Stacy said. "But can a rabbit wear a hat?"

Abby giggled. She wiggled her fingers. "Right between his ears," she said.

Stacy went to the closet. She found Sunday Funnies' bow tie. "Look what I made."

"Hey, you're good," Abby exclaimed. "Let's make everything out of the Sunday comics."

"How about a hat-fitting party tomorrow after school?" Stacy suggested. "For girl animals only."

"Double dabble good!" Abby said.

"Let's meet at the end of the cul-de-sac," Stacy said. "Between Mr. Tressler's house and the old oak tree." She followed Abby to the front door.

"It's the perfect place," Abby said as she left.

Stacy couldn't wait.

Ten

After school, Stacy measured the girl pets for their tall Easter bonnets. "Achoo!" She couldn't stop sneezing. Pet allergies were no fun!

Blinkee twitched her long bunny ears as Stacy tried to measure around them. Abby held Blinkee still.

Next was Fran the Ham. Eric bribed her with a carrot while Stacy measured. Now Stacy's eyes were super itchy!

"Achoo!" Stacy blew her nose. "This is horrible," she said.

"Here." Abby gave her a clean tissue. "Cover your nose with this."

"And try not to breathe," teased Eric.

Quacker and Snow White were last. The

tissue didn't help. Stacy's eyes watered even more.

She thought about the Easter parade—a good surprise for her father. For *all* the parents in the cul-de-sac. No way would she give up! Not even for allergies!

■■■

After supper, Stacy made herself a mask from an old T-shirt. She cut holes for the eyes. *This will keep me from sneezing,* she thought. Then she headed to Dee Dee's house.

Dee Dee giggled when she saw the mask.

Stacy measured Mister Whiskers' neck. "Bow ties look cool on cats," she teased.

Then Stacy hurried to Abby's house to measure Jimmy's duck, Jack. Dunkum and Eric went along to help.

"Bow ties look so classy on a duck," Abby said.

Jimmy held the duck's fluffy body still. Dunkum wrote down the inches on some paper.

"Simply ducky," Eric said, laughing.

Stacy smiled through the mask. She stood up to leave. Glancing across the street, she thought about Jason's slimy bullfrog and shivered. *Icksville!*

"You won't need your mask at Jason's," Abby said.

"Why not?" Stacy asked.

Eric cackled. "Frogs can't make you sneeze."

"Hey, do you know what a frog uses to cook supper?" Dunkum joked.

Jimmy shook his head. "Frog cannot cook."

"It's just a joke," Abby told her little brother.

"What *does* a frog cook supper in?" asked Stacy.

"A *croak*pot, of course!" Dunkum said, pretending to shoot a basket.

The kids giggled.

Stacy said, "Good joke, but now I've got work to do. Alone." And she wandered across the street. She held her breath inside her mask as she went.

Jason answered the door. "What's the mask for?"

"Some animals bug me," Stacy said. "I'm itchy and sneezy."

"Croaker won't bother you," Jason said.

That's what you think, thought Stacy. "What's your frog's neck size?" she asked.

Jason took the lid off the aquarium. "How should I know?"

Stacy stepped back. "Uh, don't take him out yet."

"Why not?"

"Because I don't like frogs," Stacy blurted.

Jason pushed up his glasses. "You don't?"

Stacy sat down. "I'm sorry, Jason. It's not your fault."

"That's OK. Frogs aren't for everyone."

Stacy nodded. "I guess that's why God made dogs and cats and ducks."

"Here, I'll measure Croaker's neck for you." Jason took the yellow measuring tape from Stacy.

She watched Jason touch his frog. She thought about the frog in her storybook. She tried to imagine Croaker making a deal with a real live princess.

Stacy took off her mask. Slowly, she inched closer to the green bullfrog. "Jason?"

"Yeah?"

"Will Croaker jump down the street in our parade?"

"You betcha! All you need is a fly on the end of a string," Jason said.

"He won't jump away and get lost?" Stacy asked.

"Don't worry," Jason said. "I'll catch him if he does."

Stacy carried her T-shirt mask home. She couldn't wait to find out what happened at the end of "The Frog Prince."

Maybe frogs weren't so bad after all.

Eleven

Stacy ran to her room and began to read.
The frog was sad because the princess
had not kept her promise.

One day, there was a slippery knock on
the castle door. A hoarse voice called, "Princess, princess, open up! Let me sip from your
golden cup!"

The princess ran to the door and looked
out. When she saw the frog, she almost
slammed the door. But there was a tear on
the frog's face.

"Why are you crying?" asked the princess.

"I am lonely," he said. "I want to be your
friend."

The princess began to cry, too. She was as
lonely as the green frog. "Come in. We will

have tea." And she wiped her eyes and bent down to pick up the frog.

But when she did, the frog disappeared! In its place stood a tall prince with gentle brown eyes. And he was smiling at her.

"Oh, thank you, dear princess!" The prince tipped his hat. "Your kindness did the trick at last."

The princess began to dance and sing. The prince took her hand, and they danced and sang together.

■■■

Then the doorbell rang and Stacy hurried to meet Abby. "You were right," Stacy said. "The ending is great!"

Abby sat on the floor. "It's not just a good ending, it's a good beginning, too!"

Stacy understood. In fairy tales, people live happily ever after. In real life, it's not that easy.

"It's just a story," Abby reminded Stacy. "Let's make the parade outfits."

"OK." But Stacy opened the storybook to the last page one more time.

A round gold coach with six white horses

drove up to the castle. The frog prince whisked the princess off to the royal wedding.

Stacy sighed. "My family needs some frog power."

Abby smiled. She traced the hat patterns on comic pages. "Your parents are talking to each other. *That's* a good sign. Maybe someday they'll be friends."

Stacy sat beside Abby and cut out the bonnets. With all her heart, she hoped Abby was right.

Just then, Stacy's mom knocked on the door. Quickly, the girls hid the parade stuff under the bed.

"Come in!" Stacy called when it was all clear.

Her mother carried a tray of cookies. "Are you hungry, girls?"

"Thanks," Abby said.

"Oh, this reminds me," Stacy said, taking a cookie. "I need some flies to feed Jason's bullfrog."

Stacy's mother raised her eyebrows. "Flies?"

"Frogs get hungry, too," Stacy explained.

"You could ask your father about it when he comes for supper on Friday," said her mother.

Stacy couldn't help herself. She shouted, "Thank you! Oh, Mommy, thank you!"

Of course, it wasn't gold coaches or white horses. And it certainly wasn't promises or gold necklaces. But it was *something*.

Something very special.

BOOK 6

The Mystery of Case D. Luc

To Carole Billingsley,
who solves word puzzles
faster than warp speed.
Well, almost.

One

Dunkum dribbled his new basketball up the driveway. The basketball was very special. Kevin Durant, his hero, had signed it! Kevin Durant wasn't just any basketball star. He was a Christian, too.

Jason Birchall and Eric Hagel flew into Dunkum's yard on their bikes. They skidded to a stop.

Jason dropped his bike onto the grass. "Hey, Dunk, let's ride," he called.

"Not today," Dunkum said. He aimed his ball at the net and shot. *Whoosh!* It slipped right through.

"Aw, come on," Eric begged. But Dunkum ignored them and kept shooting baskets.

Soon, Abby Hunter and her little sister, Carly, showed up. "Hi, Dunkum," Abby said.

"Do you have time to talk about the April Fool's Day party?"

Dunkum dribbled the ball under his leg. "Not now." He shot the ball up over his shoulder. It bounced off the backboard. In!

"Good shot. Now let's go," Jason said.

Stacy Henry, Abby's best friend, came down the sidewalk. "What's up?" she asked.

"Hi, Stacy," Abby said. "I'm trying to talk to Dunkum about the party next week."

Dunkum stopped shooting baskets. "Sorry, Abby. I have to keep practicing."

"But you practice *all* the time," Eric said.

Carly giggled. "If you don't watch out, you'll turn into a basketball!"

"Eric's right," Stacy said. "All you ever do is shoot hoops. What about *us*?"

Dunkum ran between Abby and Carly and shot the ball. It spun off the rim, and he chased after it.

"Stop bouncing that silly basketball," Carly said.

Dunkum froze like a statue. "What did you say?"

Jason and Eric began hooting like owls. Eric laughed so hard, his bike toppled over.

Dunkum glared at Carly. "Nobody calls my basketball *silly*! Kevin Durant wrote his name right here!" He held the ball up for them to see.

Abby shot him a sour look. "Your basketball isn't silly. *You* are!"

"Oh yeah?" Dunkum felt the back of his neck getting warm.

Stacy walked up to him. "We can't plan our April Fool's Day party because of you. You're too busy with this!" She tapped on his basketball.

Dunkum swung the ball away from her. "Then plan it without me," he said. "I don't care."

"But we always have our meetings at *your* house," Abby said. She was the president of the Cul-de-Sac Kids—nine kids on Blossom Hill Lane.

Dunkum dodged Abby, then leaped up and shot. Missed! "Go have your *silly* meeting somewhere else," he said.

Abby frowned. "Please, Dunkum. Just talk to us!"

"Not today," Dunkum said. "I'm busy."

Jason whistled. "That's what he always says!"

"Do not," Dunkum muttered.

"Uh-huh!" Eric shouted. "Maybe you want to drop out of the Cul-de-Sac Kids. Is that it?"

Abby frowned. "No, we stick together around here, remember?"

Dunkum didn't care about sticking together. His basketball was more important. He spun the ball on his pointer finger. "I'm going inside," he said, then ran into the house.

Dunkum never looked back at the other Cul-de-Sac Kids. Not even once.

TWO

In his room, Dunkum placed the ball on his dresser, in front of the mirror. He sat on his bed and stared. *Maybe this ball will make me a great player,* he thought. *Maybe I'll be as famous as Kevin Durant!*

Suddenly, he dashed to the window and pushed the curtains back. Abby and Carly were gone. So were Jason and Eric. Dunkum almost wished his friends were still waiting in the driveway.

But then he remembered the girls. They had made fun of his fantastic basketball. *Rats!* thought Dunkum. *Who needs them.*

Later, at bedtime, Dunkum read his Sunday school lesson. The verses were in Matthew 6. *Do not store up for yourselves treasures on earth . . . where thieves break in and steal. But store up for yourselves treasures in heaven. . . .*

Dunkum went to his dresser and reached for his basketball. "Maybe it's okay to store up just *one* treasure on earth," he whispered.

Then he carried the ball to his bed and pushed it down between the sheets. Dunkum crawled into bed beside it.

In the darkness, he thought about Abby and Carly Hunter. And Stacy Henry. How dare they call his basketball *silly*?

Reaching over, Dunkum felt the hard, round surface next to him. No thief was going to steal *his* treasure! Soon, he fell asleep with his arm around the giant lump.

■■■

Dunkum kicked the covers off. It was Sunday morning. His basketball was still in bed with him. The Cul-de-Sac Kids would die laughing, but he didn't care.

He showered and dressed for church. Then he hurried to the kitchen. "Mm-m, eggs smell good," he told his mother.

His dad passed the salt for the scrambled

eggs. Then he held up the crossword puzzle in the paper. "Can you solve this?" his dad asked.

"Looks tough," Dunkum said, studying it.

"Not for your dad," his mother said.

Dunkum nodded. It was true; his dad could solve anything. Especially word puzzles.

Before Dunkum ate a single bite, he prayed. He wished his parents would pray with him. He wished they would go to church, too. Sometimes it was lonely being a Christian.

Not long ago, Abby Hunter and her family were the only ones on Blossom Hill Lane who attended church. Now all the Cul-de-Sac Kids were going. God's love was catching. And Abby's van was getting crowded with kids—including Dunkum.

After brushing his teeth, Dunkum dashed upstairs to get his Sunday school lesson and Bible. The memory verse was easy. *Let's see,* thought Dunkum. *There was a treasure on earth and a thief stole it. And there was a heavenly treasure and no thief could snatch it!*

Before he left for church, Dunkum hid his basketball in the closet. He closed the door. Now his treasure would be safe. As safe as the heavenly treasure in the Bible.

Three

Dunkum hurried to Abby's house. The Cul-de-Sac Kids piled into the van. All but Dee Dee Winters.

"Where's Dee Dee?" Dunkum asked.

"Her cat is sick," Carly replied.

"That's strange. I saw Mister Whiskers outside yesterday," Dunkum said.

"Maybe he ate one of Dee Dee's cookies," Jason teased.

Carly stuck up for her friend. "Dee Dee's cookies are the best ever!"

"Seat belts, everyone," Abby's father said before starting the van.

■■■

After church, Abby's van pulled back into their driveway. Abby grabbed Dunkum's arm as they climbed out of the van. "We're having a club meeting right now! Before you start practicing your shots again."

"Make it quick," Dunkum said. His thoughts were on his new basketball.

Abby called the rest of the kids. They gathered in a circle on her porch. "Next Friday is April Fool's Day. I'm having a party after school," she said. "For all the Cul-de-Sac Kids."

"Where?" Stacy asked.

"Let's have it outside," Eric suggested.

"At the end of the cul-de-sac," Carly said.

"Yes!" said Shawn, Abby's adopted Korean brother. "Beside big oak tree."

Jason Birchall danced a jig. "What's to eat?"

Abby's eyes twinkled. She pulled a list out of her Sunday purse. "Here's the menu. Remember, it's an April Fool's Day party." She began to read. "First, we'll have ants on a log."

"Ants?" squealed Carly. "I'm not eating ants!"

"Next is silly dillies," said Abby, laughing.

"I know what *that* is," Jason said.

"Don't tell." Abby continued, "Number three is garden popsicles."

"Mm-m," said Eric. "Sounds good."

Stacy held her hands over her ears. "Don't tell me! I want to be surprised."

"Next," said Abby. "We'll have jitter blocks."

Carly giggled. "Must be something wiggly."

"Last of all, we'll have sweet hearts," Abby said.

Dunkum frowned. "I thought it was an April Fool's Day party, not a Valentine party."

"Who cares," said Jason. "Sweets are good any day."

"You better stay away from them," said Dunkum. "Remember Valentine's day, when you pigged out on chocolates?"

Jason groaned and held his stomach. He remembered.

"Hey, Abby, what are jitter blocks?" Dunkum asked.

Abby smiled. "April Fool's Day food, that's what."

Jason and Eric poked each other, laughing.

Jimmy Hunter, Abby's little Korean brother, tugged on the list. "I not like that American food."

Abby hugged him. "It's just for fun," she said. "You'll see."

Stacy grinned. "What will we do at the party besides eat strange food?"

Dunkum had an idea. "We could play basketball."

The kids groaned.

"Not *that* again!" Carly shouted.

"Then I'm not coming," Dunkum said. And he leaped off the porch and headed home.

Four

unkum's friends called to him, but he kept running. He was sick of planning parties. He was dying to practice basketball.

As he turned toward his house, he heard Dee Dee Winters calling. She lived across the street.

Dunkum spun around. "What do you want?" he grumbled.

"Come over here," she called from her front door.

Dunkum stomped across the street.

Dee Dee was holding her sick cat. "Did you get me a Sunday school paper?"

"I'm not in your class," Dunkum replied.

"Well, *I* got one for you when *you* were sick. That's what friends are supposed to do."

Then she asked, "What was your memory verse today?"

"It was two verses, Matthew 6:19 and 20," Dunkum said. "Read it for yourself."

"I already did," Dee Dee answered.

Dunkum shook his head. "Then why did you ask me?"

She grinned. "Just checking."

Dee Dee's as sick as her cat, thought Dunkum. He stormed down the steps and dashed across the street. *Ka-bang!* Dunkum slammed his front door.

Upstairs, he ran to his room and threw open the closet door. He reached for his basketball. It was gone!

Dunkum searched the back of the closet. He looked behind his overnight bag.

"Mom! Dad!" Dunkum called. He ran downstairs, darting in and out of the kitchen. He checked the family room. The house was empty.

Then he remembered. The front door was *unlocked* when he came in. "That's it! A thief walked right into my house and stole my basketball!"

Dunkum didn't bother to check if anything

else was missing. He could think of only one thing—his basketball.

Running back upstairs, Dunkum searched everywhere. He looked under his bed. Nothing.

He looked in the hamper. Nope.

He even looked behind the shower curtain. But his ball was nowhere to be found.

Dunkum fell on his bed. The lump in his throat grew and grew. He could hardly swallow. When he did, tears filled his eyes. But he squeezed his eyes shut and wiped the tears away.

He got up and marched downstairs, wondering where his parents were. Looking on the counter, Dunkum spotted a note.

Dear Dunkum,
   We'll be back in a jiffy. We went to get fried chicken. I hope you're hungry!

                        Love ya,
                        Mom

   P.S. I left the front door open. I guess you figured that out.

Dunkum put the note back on the counter. He stared out the kitchen window. "The thief might still be out there," he whispered.

He almost wished that rotten thief were lurking nearby. Dunkum would sneak up behind him. And grab his basketball right back!

Five

Dunkum leaned closer to the window. He watched for the slightest movement in his backyard. But no one was hiding in the bushes.

Then Dunkum had an idea. He would call Dee Dee. She might know something. After all, she had the best view of his house. And . . . she had stayed home from church.

Dee Dee answered the phone. "Hello?"

"Have you seen anybody hanging around my house today?" Dunkum asked.

"Nope."

"Are you sure?" he asked.

"I'm sure," Dee Dee said.

"Well, you better lock your doors."

"How come?"

"Because there's a thief in the cul-de-sac."

Dee Dee gasped. "A thief! That's horrible!"

"Yes, and he robbed my house while we were at church," he said. "I better warn the rest of the kids." Dunkum said good-bye and hung up the phone.

Next, he called Jason, who lived next door to Dee Dee.

Br-r-ring!

"Hello?" Jason answered.

"Hey, Jason, you'd better keep your doors locked. There's a thief in the cul-de-sac."

"A what?" Jason yelled into the phone.

"A thief," Dunkum said. "And he just left my house!"

"How do you know?" Jason asked.

"He stole my new basketball," Dunkum said. "The one my uncle got for me from Kevin Durant."

Jason started laughing.

"Hey! It's not funny," Dunkum said.

"I know, I know," Jason said. "It's just so weird."

"How could the thief know where I hid it?" Dunkum said.

"It's real creepy," Jason whispered. Then

he paused. "Hey, wait! I'm looking out my window. There's something blue stuck on your basketball pole."

Dunkum dropped the phone and ran outside. Jason was right! Dunkum peeled the blue paper off the pole. A bunch of dots and lines scampered across the page.

It looked like a secret code.

Who put it here? Dunkum wondered.

Then he saw a strange name at the bottom. Someone had signed it *CASE D. LUC*.

"That's weird," Dunkum said out loud. "I don't know anyone by that name." He stared at the blue paper. There was some writing at the top. It said, *IF YOU WANT YOUR BASKETBALL BACK, CRACK THIS CODE*.

Dunkum stomped his foot. "Nothin's gonna stop me from getting my basketball back!" he shouted.

Six

Dunkum saw Jason coming across the street. "Look at this!" Dunkum shouted. He waved the blue paper at his friend.

Jason pushed up his glasses and looked at the code. "I think it's Morse code."

Dunkum scratched his head. He studied the name at the bottom. "Who in the world is Case D. Luc?"

"This is crazy," Jason said.

"Can you help me crack the code?" Dunkum asked.

Jason shook his head. He had to go home for dinner. "Look in your encyclopedia," he called over his shoulder.

Rushing inside, Dunkum grabbed the

encyclopedia. He found the page with the Morse alphabet:

A • ▬
B ▬ • • •
C ▬ • ▬ •
D ▬ • •
E •
F • • ▬ •
G ▬ ▬ •
H • • • •
I • •
J • ▬ ▬ ▬
K ▬ • ▬
L • ▬ • •
M ▬ ▬
N ▬ •
O ▬ ▬ ▬
P • ▬ ▬ •
Q ▬ ▬ • ▬
R • ▬ •
S • • •
T ▬
U • • ▬
V • • • ▬
W • ▬ ▬
X ▬ • • ▬
Y ▬ • ▬ ▬
Z ▬ ▬ • •

Dunkum studied the dots and dashes on the blue paper. (Reader, can you crack the code before Dunkum does?)

    — ———

    ••—• •• —• —••

    —••• •— •—•• •—••

    •—•• ——— ——— — —•—

    ••—• ——— •—•

    ——•• •— — •

    •—— •• — ••••

    —•—• •••• •— •—•• ——•—

    —— •— •—• ——•—

    — ——— ——— —— •—• •—• ——— •——

Signed,
Case D. Luc

Dunkum found a pencil and began filling in the letters. It was easy. He could read the entire message. If his basketball was truly safe, that was good. But waiting till tomorrow for the next clue? That wasn't good. Where would he find a gate—with a chalk mark?

Boom! Thunder shook the house.

"Oh no!" cried Dunkum. "Not rain!" The chalk mark on the gate—wherever it was— might wash off.

What then?

Seven

On Monday, Dunkum woke up and reached for his basketball. He had forgotten it was gone. Sadly, Dunkum rubbed the sleep from his eyes. He ran to the window and looked out.

It was still raining!

Dunkum trudged downstairs. How would he find a chalk mark in the rain? His next clue depended on it!

■■■

After school, the rain had stopped. Dunkum wasn't going to walk home with the Cul-de-Sac Kids. Not today. He had an important mission to accomplish. A secret mission!

At home, Dunkum grabbed his after-school snack. Then he dashed outside to search for a gate. But where?

Dunkum knew of only one gate in the whole cul-de-sac. It was in Mr. Tressler's backyard. He was the old man who lived at the end of Blossom Hill Lane. The Cul-de-Sac Kids had welcomed Mr. Tressler to the neighborhood last Christmas. Now he wasn't lonely anymore.

Dunkum headed for Mr. Tressler's house. He ran past Dee Dee's house. And Jason's. And Eric's.

At last, he came to the end of the cul-de-sac. Marching up the steps, Dunkum headed for Mr. Tressler's doorbell. He rang it twice.

"Hello there, young man," the old gentleman said.

"Good afternoon," Dunkum said politely. "May I please look for something in your backyard?"

The man's face wrinkled into a smile. "Be my guest."

Dunkum thanked him and sprinted to the backyard. He headed for Mr. Tressler's back gate and searched for a chalk mark. There was no X mark near the latch. There was no X mark on either side of the gate.

Dunkum knelt in the damp grass. Then he spotted something. It was a chalky white X. "Yes!" he shouted.

Now, where was the clue? Dunkum spotted an old flowerpot. Something was sticking out of the dirt. He pulled at it, but it was only a curled-up leaf.

But wait! Dunkum could see something yellow peeking out of the leaf—a piece of paper. He opened it and found another coded message inside.

Staring at the yellow paper, Dunkum gulped. "There's no way I'll figure out *this* code," he said out loud.

"What's that you say?"

Dunkum stood up.

Mr. Tressler was calling to him from his deck. "What did you find out there?"

Dunkum ran across the yard with the yellow paper. Mr. Tressler looked puzzled when he saw the code. It was a bunch of strange shapes and symbols.

Then Dunkum told him about the missing

basketball. And the first secret code—the Morse code.

"A boy could get mighty lonely without his basketball," Mr. Tressler said. There was a twinkle in his eye.

"That ball means everything to me," Dunkum said.

"Everything? Even more than your friends in the cul-de-sac?" A surprised look swept across Mr. Tressler's face. "Seems to me a ball is a poor exchange for friendship."

"I want to be a great player someday," Dunkum said. "Just like Kevin Durant. That means I have to keep practicing."

"What's wrong with your old ball?"

"It's not the same," said Dunkum. "Kevin Durant signed my new one!"

"I see," Mr. Tressler said, raising his eyebrows. "How can that make *you* play better?"

"It's fun to pretend. That's all," Dunkum said.

"Your friends are real, though. Nothing pretend about them. . . ." The old man's voice trailed off.

Dunkum blurted out, "My new basketball is more fun!"

Mr. Tressler lowered himself into a patio chair. He faced Dunkum squarely. "Well now, how could a ball be more fun than Eric and Shawn and Abby and—"

Dunkum stood up. "I have important work to do," he said in a huff. "Excuse me." And he ran out of the yard.

When he stopped to lock the gate, Dunkum saw something strange. Mr. Tressler was grinning!

Eight

Dunkum ran next door. "Is Eric home?" Dunkum asked Mrs. Hagel.

"He's riding bikes with Jason and Shawn," she said.

Dunkum sat down on Eric's step, thinking about Mr. Tressler. *Why was he grinning like that?*

Feeling quite lonely, Dunkum trudged across the street. Maybe Abby was home. He felt a lump in his throat as he knocked on her front door. He wished he hadn't yelled at her yesterday.

The door opened. It was Abby's little sister, Carly. "Hi, Dunkum." She had a stack of construction paper in her hands.

"Is Abby home?" Dunkum asked.

"She's at Stacy's," Carly said.

Just then, Dee Dee came down the hall to sneak up on Carly. "Gotcha!" she shouted.

Carly jumped, and the stack of colored papers fell to the floor.

Dunkum helped pick them up. When he started to hand a yellow page to her, he stopped. He looked at it. "Hey, wait a minute," Dunkum whispered to himself. "This paper looks the same as the one in my pocket!"

"Talking to yourself?" Dee Dee teased.

Dunkum held up the yellow construction paper. "Where did you get this?"

"The art supply store. Why?" Dee Dee asked.

Dunkum shook his head. "Just wondered."

"Carly and I are doing a project for school," Dee Dee said. "And we're going to get an A+! Right, Carly?"

Dunkum scratched his head and turned to go.

Carly closed the door.

Dunkum pulled the yellow coded message out of his pocket. He stared at it. *Did Case D. Luc buy his paper at the same store as Dee Dee?* thought Dunkum.

Just then, Jimmy Hunter came up the walk.

"Hi, Jimmy," Dunkum said. "Can you help me?" He felt silly asking a first grader for help. But he had no other choice. Everyone else was busy.

Jimmy pointed to himself. "Me?"

"Yes, you." Dunkum held up the yellow paper. He showed Jimmy the shapes on the latest code. "Have you ever seen anything like this?"

Jimmy nodded his dark head.

"You have? Where?" Dunkum shouted. "Maybe you can help me crack this code."

"I not know about codes, but I see shapes in book," Jimmy said. "Wait!" He ran into the house. Soon, he came back with a book. "Here." He shoved the book into Dunkum's hands.

Dunkum opened the library book. There were lots of codes inside. "Hey, thanks!" Dunkum patted Jimmy on the back.

Jimmy grinned. "Open to first page."

Page one was a pictogram. Just like the code Dunkum had found in Mr. Tressler's backyard!

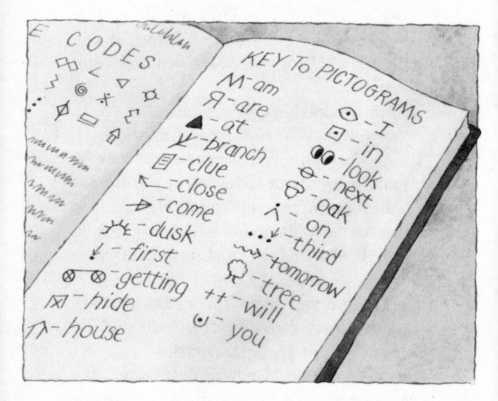

Nine

Dunkum looked at the pictogram, then at Jimmy. "Where did you get this?"

"From sister's room."

"Which sister?" Dunkum said.

"Big sister, Abby."

"What's she doing with a code book?" Dunkum said, half to himself and half to Jimmy.

Jimmy grinned. "Abby have pen pal. She write secret codes to Abby."

"Codes in a letter?" Dunkum said.

Jimmy nodded again. "Abby need book to help her read secret messages."

Dunkum stuffed the yellow paper into his

shirt pocket. He wondered if Case D. Luc knew about this book.

Dunkum thanked Jimmy and hurried home. He didn't want to forget the pictograms in Abby's codebook. Running into the house, he pulled the yellow paper out of his pocket. Dunkum began to fill in the blanks. (Reader, can you finish before he does?)

When he finished, the message was clear. Dunkum had to climb the old oak tree at the end of the cul-de-sac. Tomorrow, the next clue would be waiting—on the third branch!

But waiting was hard for Dunkum. Twenty-four hours! How could he last another day without his basketball?

He watched for Eric, Jason, and Shawn from his front window. They would be back from riding bikes soon. Maybe he would ask them to come over and play. It had been a long time since he'd seen them.

After ten minutes, Dunkum gave up. He took some paper from the kitchen. Then he sat at the table and made a list of clues. He wrote a heading on his list.

THE MYSTERY OF CASE D. LUC

1. Basketball—signed by Kevin Durant
2. Basketball—stolen by Case D. Luc (???)
3. Blue Morse code—found on basketball pole
4. Chalk mark on Mr. Tressler's gate
5. Yellow pictogram clue—found in flowerpot

6. Construction paper from art store—same as code paper
7. Library book—pictogram on first page
8. Next clue—tomorrow (in the old oak tree)

Dunkum twirled his pencil. He was determined to find this Case D. Luc person. He would never give up!

Ten

It was Tuesday—almost dusk.

Dunkum stared up at the old oak tree. He switched on his flashlight and pointed it up. He was dying to see his basketball sitting in the branches. But no basketball was in sight.

Up, up he climbed. Squatting down on the third branch, he looked around. No clues anywhere! He counted the branches again. 1 . . . 2 . . . 3! Nothing there.

Just then, Stacy Henry came by walking her dog, Sunday Funnies. She stopped under the lamppost. "What are you doing?" she called.

"Nothin' much," he answered.

Stacy walked toward him.

He wished she'd go away. He had to hunt for his next clue in private!

"Want some company?" she asked. Before he could say no, Stacy tied her dog to the tree. And she scrambled up to the third big branch.

Part of Dunkum wanted to tell her to leave. The other part wanted someone to talk to.

Soon, Mr. Tressler's porch light came on. His house was closest to the oak tree.

"I wonder if Mr. Tressler's expecting someone," Stacy said.

"Maybe," Dunkum said, glancing over at the old man's house. "He gets lonely, I think."

"Yeah," Stacy said. "I'm glad he has the Cul-de-Sac Kids to keep him company."

"I wish *I* still did," Dunkum whispered.

Stacy smiled at him. Mr. Tressler's porch light helped Dunkum see her face. "You still have us," Stacy replied.

"It doesn't seem like it," Dunkum said sadly.

"Maybe you should come to the April Fool's Day party on Friday," she suggested. "It's going to be lots of fun."

Dunkum sighed. "Maybe I will."

Sunday Funnies began to whine.

Dunkum looked down at him from high in the tree. "Hey, look! Your dog's trying to get loose," he said.

Stacy laughed. "He likes to be where the action is. And right now, that's up here."

"Why don't you go down and bring him up?" Dunkum said. "Then he won't be lonely."

"I better not. It's getting dark," she said. "My mom might worry."

Dunkum was sorry to see Stacy leave. He watched her climb down from one branch to another. Soon, she was at the bottom, looking up.

"See you at school tomorrow." She waved good-bye.

Alone again, Dunkum leaned back against the tree trunk. He looked up at the stars. He thought about the April Fool's Day party. He thought about his cul-de-sac friends. A sad feeling filled his heart.

Then Dunkum remembered why he was sitting in the tree. He looked again for the clue. In the dim light, he saw a pink note squished between two branches. *Why couldn't I find this before?* Dunkum wondered.

He opened the note and found a list of words. It looked like a grocery list. *Stacy must have dropped this*, Dunkum thought.

But where was the code?

Eleven

Dunkum scrambled down, out of the tree. He ran all the way to Stacy's house. Her mother might need the grocery list. He knocked on the door.

Stacy answered. "Hi, again."

"Did you drop your mom's grocery list?"

"What list? Where?" Stacy asked.

"In the tree." Dunkum showed her the paper.

"That's not my mom's list. Look, it has other words mixed in with the food words," Stacy said. She stared at the paper.

Dunkum looked at the list, too.

crackers	oranges	peaches
yogurt	chips	potatoes
look	salsa	after
out	your	today
tower	man	spaghetti
apples	lettuce	school
on	baked beans	soup
shirt	bike	tomorrow

"That's strange. Could this be some kind of code?"

"Maybe," Stacy said. "I saw a code like this once. My uncle made it up. He called it a jumble code."

"What's that?" Dunkum asked.

"It's easy," Stacy said. "Each word in the secret message comes right *below* the food words. The rest of the words don't count."

"Oh, I get it."

Stacy ran into the house. She came back with a pencil. "Here, let's solve it together."

Dunkum paused. "Um, not now. But thanks."

"Why can't we work on it now?" she asked.

Dunkum scratched his head. "Sorry, Stacy. I better go home."

"Aw, please?" Stacy begged.

"I'll see you at school," Dunkum said. "Bye." He felt bad about leaving his friend like that. Stacy wasn't trying to snoop. He knew she just wanted to be a good friend. But it was too late for him to be out.

Dunkum ran home to crack the code. When he finished it, the message was clear.

"Hey, wait a minute! How does Case D. Luc know I have a bike?"

"What did you say?" his mother said, coming down the steps into the living room.

"Nothin'," Dunkum muttered.

"Your friend Eric called," she said.

"He did?"

"He wants to play tomorrow."

"All right!" Dunkum shouted. "When?"

"After school." His mother grinned.

Dunkum spun around and aimed at the fireplace. He leaped up like he was shooting a basketball. He couldn't wait to see Eric again!

■ ■ ■

After school the next day, Dunkum greeted Eric. The boys rushed into the kitchen for some lemonade.

"Coming to Abby's party?" Eric asked.

"You bet!" Dunkum said.

"Changed your mind?" Eric asked.

Dunkum nodded. He didn't care about finding the next clue. It didn't matter now. Being with friends was much better.

At bedtime, Dunkum remembered the clue. Dashing downstairs, he looked in the garage. A green paper, folded like a note, was taped to his bike. Dunkum pulled the note off the seat. Strange-looking words were written inside.

EMOC OT ELOPGALF NI TNORF FO LOOHCS TA EERHT NO YADIRF. I LLIW GNIRB LLABTEKSAB.

Signed,
Case D. Luc

How did this get here? Dunkum wondered. He studied the code for a long time. Then he ran inside and held the green paper up to a mirror. The words were still mixed up.

Finally, he figured it out. The words weren't mirror image. They were backward!

The message was *COME TO FLAGPOLE IN FRONT OF SCHOOL AT THREE ON FRIDAY. I WILL BRING BASKETBALL.*

Dunkum folded up the note. The April Fool's Day party was at three o'clock, too. How could he meet Case D. Luc *and* go to the party?

Dunkum stared at the note. *What should I do?* he thought.

Twelve

It was almost three o'clock on Friday. Time to meet Case D. Luc at the flagpole. And . . . time for the party at the end of the cul-de-sac.

Dunkum sat on his front porch. He thought about Case D. Luc and the codes. He thought about the Cul-de-Sac Kids and the party. He missed his friends more than his new basketball. *Rats!* he thought. *Let Case D. Luc keep the silly ball.*

He ran to the end of the cul-de-sac. Abby smiled. "Hi, Dunkum," she said. "Didn't you hear? We canceled the party."

Dunkum stepped back. "You what?"

Abby sat on the curb. "I'm sorry, Dunkum."

"But I just talked to Eric about it the other day." Dunkum's heart was pounding. "And what about Stacy? She told me she was coming!"

"That's funny," Abby said, looking strange.

"It's *not* funny," Dunkum insisted.

Then—*tap, tap!* A familiar sound greeted Dunkum's ears. The Cul-de-Sac Kids were coming out of their houses. What's more, they were all bouncing basketballs!

Dunkum turned to Abby. "What are they doing?"

"April Fool's, Dunkum!" she said. "The party is just beginning!"

The kids ran toward the oak tree, bouncing the balls. Dunkum was glad. He'd missed his friends. A lot!

Abby grabbed Dunkum's arm. "Look! There's Case D. Luc!"

Dunkum didn't see anyone new. "Where?"

Abby giggled. " 'Case D. Luc' is 'cul-de-sac' spelled backward."

Dunkum was puzzled. "Case D. Luc isn't some guy?"

"Nope," Abby said, grinning. "The Cul-de-Sac Kids pulled a trick on you."

Dunkum couldn't believe it!

"We missed you, Dunkum. You were always playing basketball," she said. "We had to get your attention somehow."

"What a good trick," Dunkum said as he ran to meet the kids.

The Cul-de-Sac Kids grabbed him. "April Fool's!" they shouted.

Dee Dee pushed her way through. "Here, Dunkum." She gave him the Kevin Durant basketball. "I was your thief."

Dunkum scratched his head. "*You* stole it?"

Dee Dee nodded.

"But how did you find it?" Dunkum asked.

"Easy," she said. "Your mom found it in your closet. I got it from her while you were at church."

"My parents helped you?" Dunkum said.

"We *all* helped," Eric said. "I wrote the Morse code on Dee Dee's blue construction paper."

"Mr. Tressler hid the yellow pictogram in his flowerpot," Abby said.

"And I marked the X on his gate," Jason said. "After it stopped raining." He jumped up and down holding the chalk.

Abby laughed. "I found the pictogram code in my library book."

At last, everything made sense.

Shawn smiled. "Me and Stacy write jumble code."

Dunkum twirled the basketball on his pointer finger. He laughed with his friends. "I learned a good lesson. Thanks to Case D. Luc!"

The Cul-de-Sac Kids cheered.

Stacy disappeared behind a bush. She came back carrying a tray. "Anybody hungry?"

"Everyone gets a menu first." Abby gave an orange-colored menu to each kid. Jason passed around a box of pencils.

APRIL FOOL'S DAY MENU

*(Draw a line to match
the funny food with the answer.)*

Ants on a Log	strawberry Jell-O cubes
Silly Dillies	heart-shaped mints
Jitter Blocks	carrots
Garden Pops	dill pickles
Sweet Hearts	celery with peanut butter and raisins

"Hey, this is fun!" Dunkum said. He drew a line from Garden Pops to carrots. Then he chomped on one.

Abby pretended her raisins were ants—falling off the celery log and into her mouth.

Dee Dee squealed, "Oh, yuck!"

After the snacks were eaten, Abby made a suggestion. "Let's play basketball at the school."

Everyone agreed. The kids bounced their basketballs down the middle of the street. Dunkum led the way.

At the end of the cul-de-sac, Dunkum glanced over his shoulder. There was a message written on Abby's T-shirt. It said, *CUL-DE-SAC KIDS STICK TOGETHER!*

Dunkum dribbled his ball hard and fast. *Case D. Luc, you're terrific!* he thought.

Then the Cul-de-Sac Kids crossed the street to Blossom Hill School.

Together!

About the Author

Beverly Lewis thinks all the Cul-de-Sac Kids are super fun. She clearly remembers growing up on Ruby Street in her Pennsylvania hometown. She and her younger sister, Barbara, played with the same group of friends year after year. Some of those childhood friends appear in her Cul-de-Sac Kids series—disguised, of course!

Now Beverly lives with her husband, David, in Colorado, where she enjoys writing books for all ages. Beverly loves to tell stories, but because the Cul-de-Sac Kids series is for children, it will always have a special place in her heart.